Without Alice

D. J. Kirkby

Punked Books

Published in 2010 by Punked Books
An Authortrek imprint

Punked Books
C/O Authortrek
PO Box 54168
London
W5 9EE
(FAQ via www.authortrek.com/punked-books)

Dedication and Acknowledgement

This is dedicated to my husband, son and stepsons. You make my life magic and I love you all up.

I would also like to thank Dr Judith Gould who diagnosed me with Asperger's syndrome (a form of autism) when I was 40 years old. In doing so she gave me license to begin gaining a better understanding of myself.

Prologue

July 1977 Portsmouth

Fern Redwood lowered herself into the bath. As she sank to shoulder depth she firmly pushed the day's worries aside. Fleetingly she relished the sensation of the perfumed water rising up her body, warming in increments as it ascended. The tendrils of warm steam wafted away to cling onto the asparagus fern that hung down from the shelf over the toilet. Lifting her book she tried to read, wet fingers marking the pages, rivulets running down her wrists to meet the water's margin. After a moment she gave up the pretence and let her eyes drop to her belly. The swelling crested just under her belly button in an innocuous 'I ate too many mince pies at Christmas' kind of way. A casual observer wouldn't guess the secret it nurtured within. The faint red circle with a smaller dot in the centre was midway between umbilicus and pubis and lurked like a ladder in a pair of tights; painless and easily forgotten until glimpsed the next time.

Fern had woken that morning, opened her eyes and waited with resigned expectation, then grinned delightedly at the sight of the sunlight dappling through the bamboo blinds. Little did she know that this was to be the day that the edges of her world would begin to crumble. She was sixteen weeks pregnant and for once felt hunger pangs rather than tumultuous nausea. She had decided that this called for a celebratory feast and her husband Gary had happily obliged her by making a home cooked breakfast for them. Feeling sleepy from the carbohydrate and fat overdose, they had been cuddled up on the couch when the doorbell rang. Reluctantly Fern stood, pressed the palms of her hands on her hips and stretched backwards before moving towards the door.

The already familiar blue of the midwife's uniform was visible through the opaque glass of their front door and the sight made Fern's stomach flip; the nausea returning, swirling itself into a whirlpool, food floating unpleasantly on top of this internal vortex. Fern glanced over her shoulder at Gary while unlocking the door. The fear in her eyes roused him from his stupor.

'Who is it darling?' he leapt to his feet, nervously rubbing his face then running a hand through his hair.

'Hi!' Fern said, the false gaiety betraying her nervous interior. 'Please, come in. Make yourself comfortable.' Fern asked, indicating the settee and easy chairs in the front room.

'Hello,' Gary said as he stood aside to let the midwife pass like visiting royalty.

'Would you like a cup of tea?' Fern asked as the midwife settled herself on the easy chair.

The midwife declined Fern's offer of tea and then briskly demolished their dreams, with the emotionless expertise of a terrorist, 'Bad news I'm sorry to say. Your test results have come back with a 1:10 chance of Down's syndrome.'

They had sat dejectedly beside each other while she somehow made it worse by depersonalizing the bad news, discussing their baby in terms of statistics, talking to them as if she were standing at a podium in the front of a lecture theatre. In hindsight, the whole event seemed somewhat vague, like watching a horrific event broadcast on the evening news. Fern sunk into Gary turning to look up at his face for comfort. Instead she felt a ripple of adrenaline as she caught sight of her husband's eyes brimming with tears. Her eyes filled and began to sting as he squeezed her hand in an attempt to soothe.

The midwife explained that an appointment had been made for them to have an amniocentesis test in two days time. She left them with leaflets explaining about the amniocentesis and the associated risk of miscarriage which lasted for up to a month after the test. This risk hammered away at Fern's delicate emotions. This test was their only hope of a yes or no answer. When they got the results they would be expected to decide if they wanted to 'carry on with the pregnancy', as if their baby was a mere nuisance, something easily discarded.

Fern cried herself into a false sense of calm. Gary

unsuccessfully did his best to avoid thinking about it all. Neither slept much in the forty eight hours before the amniocentesis appointment. Instead Fern used the time to learn as much as she could about Down's syndrome. Gary listened as she shared all that she had managed to find out about the condition but refused to give an opinion on whether she should have the test and risk losing their baby.

'At the end of the day love, it isn't about what I want. It's your body that has to have the test done on it,' Gary said, half answering her question and absolving himself of any responsibility for decision making.

'But... do we really need to know if our baby has Down's syndrome, do we need to know badly enough to risk a miscarriage?' her pleading tone was clearly audible but Gary just shook his newspaper out forcefully and lifted it to block her attempts at eye contact.

'If you decide you want to have the test done, I'll come and hold your hand,' his somewhat muted response made its way out from behind the newspaper and put an end to the conversation.

Eventually Fern decided to look at the amniocentesis as an opportunity for them to learn more about their baby, this little person whom they had created.

Feeling giddy from lack of sleep, they had made their way into the hospital for the test. It was over so swiftly that it almost seemed a mockery of the emotional pain it had already caused. Afterwards Fern had been told to relax and rest; which was how she had come to be lying in the bath nervously flickering her eyes over the penny imprint. In its centre was that tiny red mark where the needle had passed on its way to violate their baby's privacy. Soon they would know all of their baby's secrets and in return they would be expected to decide whether they wanted to reject this little being or celebrate its uniqueness.

For the next two weeks Fern alternated between hoping the tests would give them the news they were hoping for and having to restrain herself from looking into the best ways to raise a child with Down's syndrome. The consultant had told them that they would know their baby's gender as part of the test results. Fern clung to the excitement of this part of the test result and prayed every day that he would tell them they were having a daughter. This hope sustained her in her darkest part of the night when she would frequently be awake, fretting and fidgeting. Gary, outwardly stoic, watched his wife in despair. He could hardly bear to see the woman he loved in such torment, had to push aside his own fears because he had no words to describe how he felt. Instead, he watched and waited and held her when she cried in the night.

Two weeks later Fern and Gary sat silently, exhausted, outside the consultant's office. The parade of women with their bulging bellies should have been a torment but instead they were a promise of latent dreams. Fern and Gary smiled weakly at each other. They had decided to celebrate their baby's existence regardless of the test results and were completely in agreement that every human had a right to be unique. Giving each other strength through their clasped hands, they waited expectantly, looking towards the consulting room where their baby's diagnosis awaited them.

July 1977 Bournemouth

Her first contraction had been sudden and shocking, overwhelming her as she walked the dog around the duck pond before lunch. Passing as quickly as it had overcome Sabi, the memory of that sensation followed her as she made her way home through the light rain. Out of habit rather than desire Sabi had flicked the kettle on to boil as soon as she got in. Still warm from her exertions, she had flung open the kitchen window, enjoying the smell of the rain without the accompanying discomfort she experienced outside. Convinced the contraction had been a one-off she didn't phone her boyfriend until the second one snuck up on her halfway through the cup of tea.

'Brian, it's started, come home quick,' she gasped out, breathless with excitement and anxious about the pain.

Aren't *contractions supposed to get more painful as labour progressed?* Sabi thought. *How will I be able to cope?*

'You all right love?'

'Fine, fine... just need you with me... you're supposed to time the contractions remember?' *And, hold my hand, rub my back, make it all better,* she wanted to but didn't say.

'Don't panic m'darlin, the midwife said first 'uns take their time, fill yourself a bath and I'll be home by the time you've got yourself in'.

Brian's timing had been slightly off as she was in, washed and wallowing in a tub of freshly poured warm water by the time he got home. Their day wore on, measured in increments of contraction and relaxation till the moment came for them to call their midwife to attend Sabi at home for the final time.

The midwife was now firmly ensconced in a corner of the room, warming up and quietly drinking a cup of tea. The three of them had rapidly developed a harmonious equilibrium; Sabi labouring with Brian's help and some sucks on the gas and air, the midwife unobtrusively going about her job, murmuring words of comfort and encouragement until Sabi began to push. She closed her eyes and concentrated with all her might in an attempt to push out the sensations of the aching in her belly and stinging between her legs. Jennie was born not long after.

Reaching down between her legs, Sabi shakily gathered up her daughter and cradled her. She stifled a gasp as the movement dragged the still attached umbilical cord between her bruised and swollen labia, the sting burning fiercely before fading into a pulse of discomfort. The midwife helped Sabi to latch her daughter for her first feed. She wanted to focus fully on nothing but this first experience of being a mother, the surprising weight of such a small being, the scent of the gloriously silky softness of her daughter's skin. This was a moment which she knew with overwhelming certainty she must capture in her mind forever. As Sabi drifted on the waves of love flowing between her and Jennie, her body delivered the placenta and Brian cut the cord ceremoniously; Jennie had flawlessly completed her transition from fetus to newborn. Later, after Sabi had bathed and climbed back into bed with Jennie, she asked Brian to open the window. He did so and then sat on the bed, arms around his family while the open window allowed the smell of rain to drift in.

Smiling, Brian murmured, 'There can be nothing on earth more powerful than the strength of the love in this room.' As he spoke, Jennie shifted slightly, the nipple slipping from her mouth as she fell asleep at the end of her second feed, snugly warm between her mother's skin and the soft blankets covering her back.

Sabi's eyes welled and her throat tightened with unshed tears of joy. She felt overwhelmed by the day and Brian's words. She realised that she had been blessed and that the smell of rain would forever be linked to her memory of this day.

July 1977 Southampton

Blinking into the dark Barbara tried to work out what had woken her. Unable to see anything and unwilling to blind herself further by switching on the lamp she strained to listen. Nothing audible, furtive or otherwise reached her ears. Living near the motorway meant that there was usually some noise filtering through their double glazing; although she had learned to tune it out until she wanted to hear it. Tim snorted gently in his sleep, heaved a huge sigh and began snoring loudly. Grinning, she gently prodded Tim until he turned onto his side and then snuggled up against the warmth of his back. She drifted back to sleep lulled by the rhythm of his breathing. He never used to snore but she knew now to expect it whenever he drank.

It seemed that no sooner had she shut her eyes then she jolted awake again, heart pounding. Her whole body was on high alert as she listened; distant cars swishing past on the motorway, the hum of the fridge, the boiler switching on, nothing which could have been blamed for her disrupting her intermittent slices of sleep. They had fallen into bed less than a few hours ago, both asleep mere seconds later. Barbara was exhausted by the early starts and late finishes that came with being a new mum. Tim had been tipsy enough to tell her he missed the times when they used to go to bed early so they could spend time awake curled up in each other's arms, looking at each other until sleep claimed one or both. However life had been rather hectic lately, in fact the past year had been a whirlwind and indulgences like romance had fallen by the wayside. This was Barbara's last thought before she was wafted back into the soft light sleep, aware that she had started to dream before she was completely unconscious.

Barbara was dreaming about their wedding, it had been a glorious day and it was a pleasure to be able to revisit it. The weather had been perfect, crisp and bright as it often was in the autumn. Tim had looked so wonderful in his tailcoat and wore it with aplomb. After several years of living together Barbara still thought he was a magnificent man and she was delighted that they were now married. All she'd ever wanted was for someone to love her and she was determined to continue doing whatever it took to keep Tim happy. They hadn't wanted the day to end and how many people got to truly say that about what usually ended up being a stressful summit to months of planning? At one point, desperate for a few minutes away from their friends and family who were unwittingly separating them from each other in their clamour to spend time with the newlyweds, they had snuck out the back door of the restaurant. They drifted along the seafront promenade enjoying the smell of the sea from one direction, fresh mown grass and late flowers from the other.

Barbara was wrenched from her dream. Feeling cheated she squeezed her eyes shut and breathed deeply hoping to continue from the point at which she been awoken. The last time she had dreamed this vividly had been during her pregnancy. What a time that had been with the pregnancy coming on the heels of the wedding; perhaps even during their honeymoon they liked to think when they tweaked their calculations just a bit. Barbara found the pregnancy quite exhausting and spent the first few months feeling sick. The nausea was her first sensation when she woke and her last on falling asleep. Morning sickness, she scoffed, a misnomer if she ever heard one. The feeling even invaded her restless sleep, sending her on an odyssey of seafaring dreams, the waves high and rolling. Each scent the ocean gave off was noxious to the extreme; dead fish and rotting kelp providing the high notes, brine and soggy driftwood balancing out the low notes of her dreams' peculiar fragrance.

When she became anxious that her vomiting would damage the brand new life inside her, the midwife tried to reassure her by explaining that the baby would take what it needed from her body even at her expense. This brought unpleasantly to mind, images of a little parasite residing within. Then the nausea lifted as suddenly as it had appeared only to be replaced by frequent trips to the loo to relieve her fraudulent bladder. She would wake on the verge of wetting herself, rush to the toilet and pass what seemed to be an insignificantly, pointlessly small amount. Why was her body making her lose precious sleep for that? Barbara would sleep between coming home from work and getting up to make supper and then go back to sleep not long after eating. Tim was left to his own devices and this usually involved finishing off the bottle of wine he had started at suppertime. This solitary drinking worried Barbara but when she broached the subject Tim brushed off her concerns saying he needed it to unwind. What he didn't tell Barbara was how much he was beginning to resent this creature growing inside her. His baby, that was taking over her life, taking her away from him. He was embarrassed by these thoughts and drank to quash them before joining her in bed. Tim was usually asleep beside Barbara when she woke an hour or so later for her first trip to the toilet. When she teased him about his early nights he protested that he was exhausted by her huffing when she woke and then by her sighing until she fell asleep again. Could have fooled her she thought, remembering his deep rhythmic breathing which greeted her upon waking and when returning to bed.

12

When her bladder adjusted somewhat to the pregnancy hormones she should have been able to catch up on her sleep but alas it was not to be. Each time she tried to turn over at night, it became a series of intricate shifts and nudges of her body instead of the one fluid movement she seemed to remember requiring to perform the simple manoeuvre. Later she realised that her body had been subtly, cleverly, preparing her to not only spread to accommodate and then deliver their growing baby, but also to be able to good naturedly endure the multitude of sleepless nights which would follow after the birth. How she coped with so little sleep was beyond her understanding and in time she even became used to it, often waking seconds before their baby did, hovering over the Moses basket as his eyes opened.

Barbara woke and launched herself out of bed. With fear threading ice through her veins she strode quickly down the corridor to crack open the door slightly. Holding her breath, she listened intently until she heard the sound of Stephen's breathing.

When she crawled back into bed Tim stirred and said tetchily, 'What's up with you Babs? It's barely daylight, Stephen's asleep, so why are creeping from his room?' *That boy takes up enough of your time when he's awake*, he thought.

'Oh Tim, I've spent all night waking up and then wondering why and I've only just realised what it was... the sound of silence from Stephen's room! He's slept through the night and I have never felt more exhausted.'

'Long may it continue, that's the most sensible thing he's ever done since he was born. Shame I can't say the same for you woman.' The sound of Tim's rumbling laugh followed Barbara into sleep.

Part One

One

Jennie lay legs akimbo, exhausted, enthralled and ecstatic.

'My baby's here!' she said aloud, to no one in particular.

The thrills were still coursing through her and she was starting to feel a bit sick from all the adrenaline still shooting round her worn out body. After that final excruciating and somehow simultaneously numbing push, Jennie had looked down between her legs.

At first, all she could see was the massively thick, coiled umbilical cord, gleaming whitely with those blue veins pulsing in time with her heartbeat. Oddly she felt very proud of that cord in those first fleeting post labour seconds, her mind hadn't quite begun to grasp that it was attached to the screaming, very red, baby on the bed. The midwife clamped the cord, cut it, and there to Jennie's amazement was a penis.

Jennie started sobbing, and then shouted, 'It's a boy.'

She looked around the room expecting the medical team to share in her delight but they were busy making sure her six week premature baby was fit and well. Jennie felt a physical ache at not being able to be the first person to hold him, until a tugging sensation distracted her as the midwife pulled the placenta from her body.

Equally diverting was the presence of her husband, Stephen. Why had she begged him to stay? Jennie wondered and a half smile traced her lips as she remembered how, though not for lack of trying, he had been useless during her labour. Even now he appeared to show little interest in his new son. Jennie gave an involuntary shrug as she reassured herself that this was down to the stress of her labour. The one thing that had stood out clearly over the past few months was Stephen's delight over his impending fatherhood. At the moment he was waffling on and basically making a nuisance of himself by getting in the way of the health care team as he had done throughout her labour. As always, he was impeccably dressed and had his hair styled to perfection. Although he wasn't noticeably below average height, his precise grooming, posturing and strutting walk reminded her of the little Bantam rooster her mother had in the chicken coop.

'Hey Jennie, bet you're looking forward to a shower, you look a right mess all covered in baby muck.' He hovered near her, looking at her with his distaste obvious in the set of his mouth. Pushed to the edge of her tolerance, tired, sore, overwhelmed, Jennie's eyes brimmed with tears at his casual cruelty. During her labour and delivery, Stephen had demonstrated a side of his personality that she had never seen before.

The baby doctors turned back to Jennie and Stephen, 'Your premature son is strong and healthy, would you like to hold him?'

She nodded and reached out with a smile on her face. Her son was placed in her arms wrapped in warm towels. Jennie stared then, unable to resist, she unwrapped the towels to admire her boy bit by bit. He was a bit battered looking, with thin skin, no eyebrows, or toenails. He was also the most glorious sight she had ever encountered.

Her voice trembled as she said, 'Can I keep him?'

Two

Stephen shuffled up along the bench to make room for a woman in her nightdress and slippers. She had an anorak hung over her shoulders to keep out the light drizzle and a bag of clear liquid hanging from a pole on wheels. He watched, shocked, as she rolled a cigarette and cadged a light from him. He passed her his lighter, too depressed to comment on how revolting it was to see a woman in her condition smoking. When she had finished using his lighter he lit his own cigarette with it before putting it back inside his pack of fags and took a sip of his tepid coffee.

This should be the happiest day of my life! He moaned inwardly, anxiety and disappointment echoing in the recesses of his mind. Fifteen minutes ago he had been with his wife as she gave birth to his first child, a boy, a baby boy. His son and heir. He felt that he had been as much a part of the labour as Jennie. He'd done his best to help the midwife in many ways, mopping Jennie's brow, rubbing her back even when she pretended to sleep and offering words of encouragement and helpful advice. Stephen was proud of the efforts he'd made to reduce the tension in the room with his own unsubtle brand of humour. He wasn't one to complain as a rule but he felt it was a shame that no one had taken the time to show his efforts had been appreciated. Now he felt angry, critical, almost rejected as he thought back over the last moments he was in the room.

'Hope your man gets treated better than I did!' he said to the woman at his side.

'Uh?' she grunted around the smoke streaming from her nostrils.

'After the doctors had finished checking my squalling little man, the midwife, who I had to put up with the entire time my wife was in labour, couldn't get me out of the room fast enough.' He shook his head. 'I mean what's all that about?'

The woman shrugged and shifted herself until she had settled her back against the bench with her legs stretched out in front, the mound of her stomach rising like an island amidst a blue terry towelling ocean.

'"Why not grab a cup of coffee while we finish off here?" she said to me. Did I say to her I wanted a coffee?'

'Dunno, did ya?' said the woman on the bench, amused.

'No I bloody didn't. What I said was, "Don't be absurd woman, I want to spend time with MY little man and obviously Jennie can't cope on her own! Just look at all the squinnying from her when she was in labour! What would she have done without my help and advice? Huh?"'

'Sounds like you were a great help to your missus. My first labour was scary. Dunno why I fell for another, must be mad. I'm ask'in for an epidural from the first pain this time 'round, can't be do'in wiv all that natural birthing them midwives keep banging on about!'

Stephen, didn't answer as he was lost in thought remembering the scene.

The midwife had pressed her lips together for a moment after Stephen's outburst before saying, 'Well if you put it that way then you definitely deserve some time on your own. Why not treat yourself to some fresh air? You've earned some peace and quiet after all *your* hard work haven't you? Jennie needs some stitches as she has a bit of a tear and then I'll help Jennie get cleaned up. Your sweet boy is asleep right now so he won't know you've popped out for a few minutes.' The midwife had managed to paste a smile on her face that she might as well of cut from a magazine and held in front of her lips, for all the effect it had on Stephen.

'Put an extra stitch in her wud'ja?' he chuckled to himself as he left, flinging a cheeky grin over his shoulder to show her that he was joking. All he got in return was a filthy look.

The woman beside him began a loud conversation on her mobile, shaking Stephen from his reverie. He took a long pull on his cigarette then flicked the butt into the gutter. He hunted into his pocket for a stick of gum to hide the smell of his fag. Jennie had no idea he'd started again, she'd been pleased as punch when he'd given up months before and that little evasion had earned him lots of "house points". That wasn't the only thing he'd "neglected" to tell her either.

Stephen smirked at the concrete and then shook his head. Sometimes he felt ashamed of his behaviour, sometimes he didn't. He had decided to cover his ass and to tell her everything months ago. Although he had plenty of opportunities, he had never gotten around to divulging the whole truth. Fear that she might leave him and take away their child had so far nibbled away at any budding intent to tell her.

A few days ago, Stephen had decided he was going to take Jennie out for dinner and tell her everything he had to tell, a problem shared was a problem halved, or so he'd heard somewhere. He thought that she'd understand, she was always very reasonable when they saw instances like this on TV shows. He convinced himself that really he could explain everything and make her understand why it wasn't his fault. He figured that a restaurant full of people would serve to keep Jennie from making a fuss and he'd make sure he took as long as he needed to make her understand before they left. No sooner had he booked the table and ended the call, his mobile rang with Jennie shrieking the news that her waters had broken and they were going to have their baby early. Promising to meet her at the hospital he went to tell his boss why he would be leaving early. Stephen fumed inwardly as he walked, thinking how it was typical of Jennie to get stuck in and screw up all his plans. Sighing, Stephen shifted on the bench and began fretting that he would never be able to tell Jennie because the likelihood was that he could lose his new little man and that was a risk he wasn't willing to take. He decided that he'd missed his window of opportunity. He knew he was stuck in a fur lined rut; unable and more than a bit reluctant to find an adult way out.

'You made your bed dickhead, better get comfy 'cos you're in it for the long haul,' he muttered to himself causing the woman slumped beside him to flick him a puzzled look as she edged away before responding to something someone on the other end of the phone had said to her. Stephen pushed himself off the bench and, stomach disturbed by a surge of indigestion; he burped, spat his gum into the hedge and headed back inside the maternity unit.

Three

Jennie was put into the only single postnatal room on the ward. She wondered why but did not voice her question aloud in case they thought her ungrateful. When they were still in the delivery room, the baby doctors had made a joke of her questioning if she was allowed to keep her son.

'Of course! You grew him, you keep him,' they laughed.

'Oh!' Jennie pressed her lips together in an anxious line, trying to piece together a coherent train of thought. 'I only meant that I thought all premature babies had to go in those things that look like fish tanks?' Jennie explained then cast an embarrassed look at the floor, not willing to make eye contact in case she didn't like what she saw reflected back.

'Some babies at this age do have to spend some time in an incubator but your son is a good weight. He'll be better off in your room, within arm's reach of your cuddles and we'll help you keep a close eye on his well-being.'

'What about his eyebrows and toenails? Will he never have any now that he has been born without them?' Jennie's voice trembled on the last sentence.

'They'll grow in their own time, not to worry; he just needs to catch up. By the time he reaches the age when he should have been born, everything will be in place. We'll come back and check on him again tomorrow, if you're worried before just let the staff know.' They dropped all their words near Jennie like several heavy suitcases and then they left the delivery room.

Jennie paced the floor of her postnatal room, cuddling her raging bundle of baby boy. Perhaps this was why she'd been allowed to keep her premature son with her Jennie thought. *Otherwise I night have exhausted myself by going back and forth to the newborn unit to sooth him, instead of exhausting myself by trying to sooth him here*, she thought wearily. *At least I can cuddle him, what a nightmare it would be if he had to be in an incubator like I thought and I couldn't hold him when he cried!* Her heart clenched tightly at this thought as if she could keep it from coming true at any time in the future by sheer physical force.

The single room was tiny and had the furniture placed in the most awkward positions possible. Immediately through the door was the side of her bed with its headboard against the middle of the back wall. The bed's proximity to the door meant that the door could only be opened three quarters of the way. However, there was only enough room for a nursing chair between the other side of the bed and the window. To the left of the door was a huge wardrobe, with both the full-length mother and pint sized baby sections still mostly empty. She could hear the hangers jangle when she walked by; at least she could whenever her son paused for breath.

The attached toilet room had a bidet. Next to it on a shelf was a stack of light green paper hand towels, some latex gloves and toilet cleanser. For cleaning the bidet before use, she assumed. The midwife who'd escorted her to the room recommended that she clean it, fill it with warm water and wee into it to reduce the sting on her tear. *Reduce? That's all? How 'bout render the pain non-existent? That'd be nice, I've had quite enough pain down there recently, thank you very much,* Jennie thought with a wince.

Like the labour ward, the decor was dire; industrial green walls rose to greet stained white ceiling tiles in a very unpleasant fashion and dropped to a sudden end at the grey speckled linoleum. The whole room had a taint of antiseptic which Jennie found vaguely reassuring, as if the smell itself could protect her little boy from the horrors of infection. Jennie thought to herself anxiously as she shuffled her slippers over another circuit of her room, worried about lifting her feet in case she slipped while carrying him. His crying made her anxious and sparked off a kaleidoscope of minor frets. *Why isn't he comforted by my cuddles? Does his skin look yellow or was that just the dim lighting? How long will it take till the baby doctor came back to check him again as promised?* Her frantic brain worked its way through these niggles, churning them over like a plough through spring soil, she searched for further concerns that she might have missed on the first pass through the fertile landscape of her imagination.

At long last, the wails diminished in volume. His chest hitched a few times, a few more cries escaped, now feeble and heart wrenching instead of deafening. His rigid body gradually relaxed against her chest and she lifted his face near hers to reassure herself that he was still breathing. The warm, gentle wisps of his exhalations against her cheek made her heart relax and then swell with painful love. She gingerly placed her now sleeping son into his cot, feet to foot the way she'd been shown, tucked his blanket in and then she lowered herself onto her bed, wincing at the sensation of the brick like wadding between her legs. The packaging had erroneously described it as a maternity pad but she couldn't feel anything resembling the comfort of padding.

The window, which reached from the ceiling to the top of the thigh high radiator, offered little more than a view of the cigarette ends which littered the courtyard which was circled by the maternity unit and the men's surgical ward. Women with either swollen bellies stretching their maternity smocks or with blood on their dressing gowns, sat spread legged on the benches or wandered around sucking smoke into their pregnancy strained lungs. The very sight probably did a lot to speed the men's recovery and discharge home from the surgical ward. It certainly repulsed her and she was an ex smoker who still missed the gentle buzz provided by nicotine. However, there was no way she would ever expose her delicate boy to all those toxins and she couldn't understand how any mother could. Jennie was aghast at the number of pregnant women she saw smoking. *How could a cigarette be more important than time with their babies? Surely getting an unborn baby addicted to a drug was akin to child abuse?* Jennie thought. She'd always felt strongly about this and even more so since she'd experienced the undeniable sensation of her own baby moving around inside her, asserting its existence.

Jennie got up to pull the blinds shut and felt the weight of her body sink her side of the mattress as she lay back down.

She had gained an enormous amount of weight during pregnancy mostly due to the fact that she craved and ate huge amounts of sweets each day. She hoped that it would all effortlessly drop off as her cravings had disappeared already. Before she had been tall enough to be considered curvy but not fat, now she was fat and not at all curvy. Her eyes remained her best feature, green-blue (hazel, her mum called them) and fringed in lashes so long they looked false when mascara was applied. She fingered her hair, it was lank and she knew the blonde highlights Stephen had talked her into didn't suit her. She was thirty-four years old, time to act her age and choose a hair colour that was flattering instead of trying to appease her husband. She made a firm decision to ask her hairdresser to give her a short cut and dye it back to its original light brown. A change would do her a world of good, in fact Jennie decided, she could do with a change of pace. It had been a whirlwind of a year and she had definite plans to make the most of her maternity leave and indulge in some down time with no responsibilities except caring for her son.

She flinched as some midwives walked past her door, chattering to each other nosily. Their staff room was adjacent to her single room. Each time the quiet of her end of the corridor would be violated for the length of their break. Previously, their sudden noise had disturbed her baby, making him cry louder, though how he could hear anyone over his own noise was a mystery to Jennie. She got up and impatiently hovered over her new son's crib, wanting to be the first thing he saw when he woke. He had only been asleep a short while and already she was desperate for him to wake so she could cradle him in her arms. Then the realisation that he was hers and she could cuddle him awake or asleep enchanted her. She lifted him from his cot and the smell of him and his weight in her arms made her soul sing. *What is it about newborns that make them smell so gorgeous?* she marvelled. Her little boy was six weeks premature and weighed almost five lbs. It scared her to think how many "pounds of ouch" she would have had to push out if he had stayed inside her for another six weeks.

So far she had only breastfed him once but the midwife on duty tried to reassure her that newborns could go quite a while without food during their first day of life. This attempt failed miserably. Everything to do with motherhood seemed a worry right now and she felt twitchy and anxious instead of glowing and serene, as she had expected. The responsibility of motherhood was overwhelming and frightening and she desperately wanted Stephen to hold her and tell her he loved her. She was fairly sure he wasn't proud of her, judging by his barely concealed contempt that had seeped out in increasing quantities while she was in labour. When she felt up to it she was going to ask him about his behaviour in the labour room, there had to be a good explanation. Jennie wondered again what had caused this change. Perhaps he couldn't cope with seeing her in so much pain. If that was the case then maybe she'd see a return of the happy-go-lucky man that she'd fallen in love with.

How Jennie wished her mum were there with her today. Her reasons for telling her to wait so long before flying over for a visit seemed ridiculous to Jennie now. She had thought it would give her time to get into a routine, to be able to show her what a good mum she was. Obligingly her mum had booked a plane ticket for three months after her expected delivery date. Jennie now realised her mother must have been crushed with disappointment at not being invited to be present for the whole scenario from first labour pain onwards and marvelled at how she had managed to not show this to her. Her mother had managed to be there anyway, in her own way, from the second contraction.

After Jennie's waters had broken she'd had to stay in hospital for twenty four hours to make sure she didn't go into labour and to have jabs to ripen her baby's lungs in case she did start contracting. She found the hospital so noisy and desperate from lack of sleep she begged them to allow her home, promising to return immediately if she started labouring. The consultant agreed that, as she only lived a five minute drive from the maternity unit, she could go home and "await events". Nothing happened the first day she was home and Jennie caught up on her missed sleep not knowing that it would be the last proper rest she'd get for a long time. She went into labour a day later at four in the morning. Jennie could remember in intricate detail the experience of being woken by her first contraction, then lying there wondering what it was that had just happened to her. She decided that anything so entirely whole body consuming, had to be a contraction. She was excited that the muscle spasm type pain had passed and got up to drink some raspberry leaf tea and make wholemeal toast with honey. If she was going into labour she wanted to have fully stocked energy stores. Spreading butter thickly on the toast, she flinched as the phone rang, and then hastily answered it, knowing that at four in the morning it could only be her mother.

'Jennie?!' shrieked her mother's voice. 'Are you in labour?!'

'I don't know mum,' said Jennie not even bothering to question how her mother knew to phone at just the right time, she guessed all mums were like that at times like this. Would she ever grow to become a mother of this calibre? She could only hope, as she felt that she certainly hadn't demonstrated this ability to herself as of yet. She had been chatting to her mum an hour later when Stephen had come down in a bad mood. He later told her it was because she hadn't woken him up to share in the excitement of the contractions she'd had while on the phone. He stormed around and then out of the house, in what Jennie assumed to be an aggressive bid for her attention. It hadn't worked though as she was still wrapped in the warmth of her mother's voice when he came slinking back in.

Tears welled in her eyes as she reflected on Stephen's behaviour. He'd become increasingly morose those past few months, reluctant to engage with her unless the activity related to their baby. The man she'd fallen in love with emerged whenever it came to preparing for their unborn child. Nursery supplies shopping, painting the walls, assembling the rocking chair, folding baby clothes into tiny bundles which filled the dresser drawers surprisingly quickly, Stephen had ensured he was involved at every step. After the birth he had withdrawn from her even further. Jennie was exhausted, anxious, lonely and terrified that Stephen no longer loved her. She placed their son back in his cot, sat on the bed and gazed at the blurry image of her dream child sleeping restlessly. His arms twitched and his hands splayed out in trembling movements before they drifted back to his mattress. She too wanted sleep, she'd had almost none in twenty four hours and her ability to cope was fading fast. She closed her eyes and willed her clenched jaw to relax; feeling heavy clouds of sleep roll over her as she did so.

Four

Stephen rang the ward doorbell. He sneezed for what seemed like the millionth time since leaving the car with his armload of flowers. The admiring looks of the women in the shop when he'd bought them had just about made it worth it but now that the attention had waned, his ego had deflated and his impatience with the awkward, irritating bundle of flowers was increasing.

For fuck's sake, how long's it going to take them to open the door? He looked pointedly to where the midwives were sitting and talking in their corner station. His favourite acid stare had no effect so Stephen then freed a hand from the flower stems and thumped his fingertips rhythmically against the glass, fixing his "bored as fuck" look in place.

A midwife opened the door with a smile, 'Hi! Sorry for the wait, we were just finishing morning duty hand over. Who have you come to see?'

Stephen told her, expecting instructions on how to get to her room but instead she walked with him and then knocked on the door and asked if Jennie wanted a visitor. What was with these "madwives" anyway? Of course his wife wanted his company, Stephen thought as he pushed past the midwife and planted a big smooch on Jennie's cheek. Christ she looked a right mess, hair all over the place, still in her nightgown and looking as if she had another baby inside her ready to come out. Stephen couldn't suppress a little shudder as these thoughts ran through his mind.

'Hiya missus, when does that go then?' he plonked the flowers on a plastic chair between the door and wardrobe and pointed at her belly as he walked past her to peer into his son's cot at the foot of the bed.

Jennie sighed and picked up the flowers. The velvet soft, pink streaked flower heads had been leaning at a precarious angle against the wardrobe. She softened as she realised he'd thought to buy her favourite, Star Gazer lilies. She looked at Stephen who was utterly absorbed by the sight of his son and breathed deeply as she clutched the flowers to her chest in lieu of a hug from her husband; each inhalation filled her brain with swirls of their heady sweet pink scent. They reminded her of marshmallows.

'I only gave birth yesterday Stephen; it took me seven and a half months to get this size so I expect it will take more than twenty four hours to go away!' She could hear the conciliatory tone to her voice and was furious with herself for it. Why did she feel obligated to make excuses for looking like she'd just given birth?

'No! Don't!' Jennie shrieked as Stephen reached into the cot to touch their sleeping son. 'He only went to sleep about half an hour ago Stephen. I'm exhausted and feel grubby. Why can't you leave him where he is? At least until I've had a shower and some breakfast?' Jennie felt guilty as soon as the words were out of her mouth. What kind of way was that to be speaking to the father of her child? No wonder he was disappointed with her.

'Stephen I'm very…' Jennie started to apologise, wanting to explain that she was desperate for some quiet time before their baby absorbed all her attention yet again. She knew that once their son was awake she would not be able to leave him, could not bear to leave him in fact but Stephen barked out a response before she could finish.

'Christ woman, if he woke up, he'd soon go off to sleep again as soon as he realised it was his daddy's arms he was lying on!' Stephen's face crumpled under the weight of his wounded pride.

'Please! Let's not fight…' Jennie's voice trembled on the last word and she pushed past Stephen to collect her bath things.

She managed to get to the bathroom and waited until the water was flooding into the tub before she sat on the chair, bent her head into her towel and howled until she had released her pent up misery. She didn't want red eyes to give away the fact that she'd been crying in case it made Stephen feel bad and so Jennie forced herself to stay in the bath with a cold washcloth pressed against her eyes until they felt less swollen. Stephen stood in the corner of the room, arms crossed, scowling, *Nice for some to be able to swan off for a luxurious bath while I'm left on my own. She's got some front trying to accuse me of starting a fight. A fine welcome that was! Lord knows I've got good reason for feeling a bit glum.* Aware he was acting like a prat only made him feel worse. Stephen spent the rest of the visit sulking, speaking in monosyllables and feeling very, very sad.

Jennie was silent with exhaustion and beyond coping with his emotional blackmail. When Stephen left, announcing he was going to the pub to "wet the baby's head with the lads", she felt a vague sense of relief mixed with a flicker of guilt. Her sweet boy was still asleep and she wanted to make the most of the opportunity to lie down with her eyes closed for as long as he allowed her. The midwives had said that he would probably get the hang of feeding that night so she didn't expect to get much rest through the night. Stephen would have to sort his own mood out; she just didn't have time to baby him any longer.

Five

The next afternoon, feeling wretched and a bit guilty, her mind continuing its expedition into this world of new mummy anxiety, Jennie stared at her boy, sleeping in his incubator. His skin had gone a bit yellow and the blood sample the midwife had taken from his heel had shown that he had jaundice. Much to Jennie's relief she was allowed to have the incubator in her room instead of having to lose him to the sick baby unit.

'There's nothing wrong with him that a few days of phototherapy won't cure.' The midwife had said cheerily as she showed Jennie how to cover his eyes and how to open the side so she could take him out for feeds and cuddles.

Jennie was convinced there was something wrong with him besides the jaundice. He wasn't seeking her out with his eyes like she'd seen other newborns do. *Am I doing something wrong? Is my sweet boy lonely for his twin?* Just the thought of that wrenched at Jennie's gut. She wanted to have a magic mother's wand that she could wave over him to make everything perfect in his world. His world that had changed so abruptly, so early in his life.

During the short time that Jennie and Stephen were aware that they were expecting two babies, they had chosen the names Marcel and Maurice. No girls names and no tempting second choices for boys names, simply Marcel and Maurice right from the very start.

Stephen, hung over, cross and scratchy, had been in a sulk during most of his visit that morning and unwilling to accept his share of the responsibility of deciding which of the names should be given to their surviving son.

'Stephen. He is two days old! The poor boy should have a name and we've had two picked for months now! I shouldn't have to do this by myself!' Jennie brought her feet up onto the footstool as she said this, wrapping her arms defensively around her stomach where her waist used to be. Stephen, from his supine position on the hospital bed said not a word in response. Instead he closed his eyes and help up a hand in that "speak to the hand 'cos my ears ain't listening" way, which he knew never failed to infuriate her.

'Why are you behaving like this Stephen? Don't you *care* if your son is nameless? Don't you *love* him enough to name him?' Jennie regretted the words as soon as they left her mouth but didn't apologise. Calmly, almost analytically, she wondered why she wanted to hurt Stephen. Momentarily, she considered whether she was going a bit mad before discarding that idea for the rubbish it was. She glared at Stephen. 'Answer me damnit!'

Stephen fidgeted, then flung himself upright, swung his legs over the edge of the bed and sat there, facing the closed door, his rigid back speaking volumes, 'What if we get it wrong, huh?'

'What do you mean honey?' Jennie's relief that Stephen was talking at last was so great that she got up from her chair and moved towards him before her pride could hold her back. She sat on the bed, facing the window, her back to his.

'I mean,' Stephen took in a long breath and said very quickly, in almost a whisper, 'what if we choose the name that his brother would have wanted? Sometimes when I'm holding him, loving everything about him, I feel guilty that I don't miss his brother more. I feel like it's unfinished business.'

Jennie swallowed around the lump in her throat, unable to respond to the perfect truth in Stephen's words.

'Yeah I know, it's a stupid thought, you don't need to answer.' Stephen's voice was harder now.

Jennie leaned back onto Stephen's back, 'No,' she said. 'No it's not even a tiny bit stupid.' Her voice broke. 'I think it's the most important thing you've said for days and I'm scared too.'

They were both silent for a few moments.

'But,' Jennie said eventually, 'we're parents now and we've got to be brave enough to do what's best for our son. We can't let fear hold us back; we need to be strong for him. He deserves a name, an identity of his own.'

'Yeah, you're right Jennie. Not today though, ok? I'm

tired.' Stephen's voice sounded sad and confused. He said his goodbyes to them both, kisses all over each of his son's tiny hands and a quick peck on the cheek for Jennie instead of the hug she'd stepped towards him for. She managed to convince herself that the relief which blossomed on his face as he stepped towards the door was from unburdening himself about his fears over the naming.

Aware she was acting slightly odd but obsessed with somehow allocating a name; Jennie then queried every person working on the ward as to which name they preferred. One midwife emphatically wrote the two names on scraps of paper, put them in a cup and took them away with her, promising a decision soon. After duty handover she had popped back declaring the name Marcel had been picked out of the cup by the ward sister. Overwhelmed by this kindness, this show of support when she felt as if all her foundations had been taken away, Jennie thanked the midwife, tears welling in her eyes. Her emotions seemed to have been completely rewired by her pregnancy and birth. Joy and trepidation jousted relentlessly in the pit of her stomach. *What kind of parents will we make if we can't even make a simple decision like choosing our son's name?* She left a message on Stephen's phone about the naming of their son and deliberately omitted to reel off her worries about their capability as parents. That wasn't the kind of message he needed to hear electronically. From what he'd told her there was a lot of worrying going on inside of Stephen anyway. Jennie sighed and tried to prepare herself mentally for Marcel's next feed. Breastfeeding didn't feel very natural, not unless you were a masochist, she thought grimly. She had never experienced pain like it. *White hot is the only way to describe it*, she'd think as he latched on and the flames of pain blossomed again. Sweat had beaded on her forehead and her feet were frantically tapping on the floor by the time Marcel had numbed her enough with his frantic suckling for her to be able to focus again. The midwife had said she should leave her breasts exposed after she'd finished feeding Marcel.

'It gives them a chance to heal, rub a little of the milk on and leave them to dry before putting them away,' she'd said in a patronizing tone, treating Jennie to what appeared to be an attempt at a reassuring smile.

No way was she going to do that! Not with Stephen making juvenile rude comments. He'd already made a comment about what he described as her "one inch nipples" and said that he'd like to have a go on them, just like his lucky little man. Jennie had shrieked in disgust, feeling repulsed and embarrassed at such inappropriate talk.

Stephen has immediately become defensive and retorted, 'Oh take a chill pill woman! Did they throw out your sense of humour with the after birth?'

Jennie decided she'd rather put up with the pain when Stephen was visiting them than offer him opportunities to make further comments and/or sneer at her. Jennie wouldn't see Stephen for a couple of days now as he'd had to go away with his work and she couldn't decide if this made her feel lonelier or relieved that there would be a couple of days without arguments.

A short while ago, Jennie had caught a glimpse of Marcel's flawless tongue; pink and tiny with hundreds of taste buds standing out in sharp relief. She waited and watched in wonder until he yawned before drifting off to sleep, displaying that perfect tongue again. For some reason the perfection of Marcel's tongue made Jennie think of the imperfections of her marriage and she began sobbing, wishing someone, anyone would hear her and come in with a magic solution to her despair. Jennie wailed silently so she wouldn't disturb Marcel.

Stop this you stupid woman, she shrieked at herself and shook her head vehemently. *What's the matter with me anyway? Here I am with a gorgeous baby that I wanted so desperately and all I can do is cry whenever he is asleep. Ungrateful that's what people will think I am, selfish and ungrateful!* Jennie had a new worry to pick at now.

Wiping her tears on a wad of the crunchy green NHS hand towels in the dispenser over her sink, she stepped over to the incubator where Marcel lay and rested her eyes on the sight of him. How did someone so perfect come out of a frantic, fumbling, alcohol induced and lust driven encounter between herself and Stephen? Jennie blushed faintly in shame at this memory. She had once been certain that it took joyous intent and loving devotion to produce such a miracle. Now she was no longer certain of anything. She was interrupted from her reverie by a knock on her door.

'Hello? Come in,' Jennie called softly hoping not to disturb Marcel's sleep.

'Mrs Copeland, PC Stowerby needs to speak to you.' The midwife pushed the door open all the way to reveal the policewoman standing behind her.

Six

It was one in the morning when Jennie had returned to the maternity unit. Earlier in the evening the police had turned up to say her house had been burgled. Stephen was away with work, unable to avoid this two day trip and said that this meant he could have a few days off when she was discharged from hospital. Their neighbours had gone in to feed their cat his evening meal and found the house a mess and Loopy cowering under their bed. By the damage done to the window in Marcel's room, it was torn off its hinges; it appeared that was how they'd gotten in. Everything with any cash-in-hand value was gone. The worst of all of this fiasco, somehow, was that Stephen hadn't answered when she had phoned his mobile to pass on the news and ask him to come home. He hadn't mentioned that he'd be impossible to contact when he phoned her for a quick chat earlier in the evening. Jennie was fuming. If he had been planning to go out partying after work, the least he could have done was warn her he wouldn't hear his phone so she wouldn't worry.

Worrying she certainly was. Worried that Stephen may have decided that his hasty marriage was a big mistake and equally worried that the stress of being a new father may have caused Stephen to pack his bags and run. For some time now, Jennie had a sense of him being pulled from them though for what possible reason she could not define. Jennie loved being part of a conventional family unit, she'd had little enough of that in her own childhood and was determined to do everything she could to ensure they stayed together. Her marriage might not be perfect but it was hers and she was willing to work as hard as she had to in order to make it last.

She'd had to go home to talk to the police, sort insurance paperwork and all the other mundane duties associated with the unexpectedly shocking violation of being robbed. She'd left Marcel, in his incubator under the watchful eyes of the unit staff with a supply of expressed milk in the fridge, should he wake for a feed while she was gone and sank into the police car feeling an unexplained sense of guilt and relief that no one saw her getting into the vehicle. The PC had accompanied Jennie through the house as she tried to work out what was missing, which was not an easy task as Jennie's house was filled with a wild profusion of fabrics which were draped over chairs, falling in lush folds from curtain rails and folded on the couch. Rich green foliage breathed life to this organised chaos, hanging from homemade macramé hangers which had beads and shells cleverly wound into the pattern of the plant holder. Many inspirational and beautiful works of art adorned the walls of her home, which she thought gave a cosy effect but which Stephen said he found stifling. Trailing ferns shadowed shelves which bulged with a well thumbed assortment of reading material and delightful flowering arrangements added their own charm; placed just so on a rickety wooden ladder. PC Stowerby's partner took notes and sketched diagrams of the crime while Jennie rummaged around in her safe for the insurance documents and cried.

The destruction was deplorable. *Why did they have to vandalize as well as steal?* Jennie wondered. *Wasn't the theft bad enough?* Before the intrusion she felt her house had been wonderful beyond all imagining, rich with vibrant colours, delightful art and luxuriant foliage. Now graffiti was scrawled on the fridge with the sponge from the shoe polish, the empty pot squashed on the tiles below.

You make it or break it in life - Im broke
I woz here when you wosnt
Fanks for everyting

Jennie read and then wished she hadn't. She averted her eyes from the rest of the scrawls. Their white walls had scrapes along the stairwell, possibly left by the TV as the thieves had carried it down from the guest bedroom. Their plush light blue carpets were covered in mud and what looked suspiciously like grease and car oil. Her jewellery had been flung around the bedroom; it had taken her ages to admit that she couldn't think clearly enough to figure out exactly what was missing from the family heirlooms she had inherited. Her Grammie Gidgit's pearl earrings were definitely gone and that upset her so much that she couldn't manage to think her way through the rest of her treasured stash of accessories.

PC Stowerby placed a hand on her shoulder and said, 'No rush, send me a list in a few days time'.

Jennie looked up from her sitting position on the bed, nodded and felt her eyes brim hotly with tears, 'Thanks. Sorry... I'm just...'

PC Stowerby's voice was gentle as she said, 'Tired? Overwhelmed? I remember feeling a lot of both when my sister was born and I didn't have to do any of the nighttime feeds or contend with my house being broken into. Don't feel you need to apologise for anything. Let's walk through the rest of your house and see if you notice anything else missing and then I'll run you back to Titchfield General.'

Their CD collection was significantly depleted and again Jennie was told to compile a list at her leisure and get it to them when she was done. The stereo was gone and to add insult to injury so was her car.

'The culprits must have found the key fob for your car,' PC Stowerby's partner said.

Jennie sighed, 'That wouldn't have been difficult I'm afraid. We hang our keys here.' She said indicating the three small hooks to the left of the front door. 'Mine, Stephen's and our bike keys.'

'They probably used your car to haul everything away.'

'But how did they know which car was mine?' said Jennie perplexed.

'Your key fob was on the hook. They leaned out the door, pressed the button to deactivate your car alarm, took note of which car's lights flashed and then loaded the stuff in. Thieves are often more clever than people give them credit for!' PC Stowerby's partner's matter of fact manner, seemingly laced with undertones of admiration for the clever criminals, grated on Jennie's jangling nerves.

'The knowledge that strangers have broken into our house, stolen our stuff, made a bloody mess and then drove off in my car makes me feel unclean by proxy; violated and insecure.'

'That's what separates you from the perps who did this to you. You're entitled to victim support, here's a leaflet with the contact details on it. We've finished here for now and it is up to the "scene of crime" team to take over now. They'll dust for fingerprints and whatnot. Let's get you back to that son of yours.'

Jennie's exhaustion was nearly overwhelming as she made her way along the corridor to her room on the postnatal ward. The hours between nine at night and one in the morning were the only guaranteed time frame that she could count on Marcel allowing her to catch up on much needed restorative sleep. She cast a loving glance at her sleeping son and then crashed into sleep as soon as her body went horizontal under her covers.

She woke with a start, sat on the edge of the bed, heart pounding sickeningly. Looking at Marcel through the incubator glass, she noted that he had done a wee while they slept. Lying naked and on his back meant that the wee covered a very large area of the incubator sides and roof as well as his face and genitals. She cleaned his little face, genitals and the incubator, proud that she managed the task on her own with ease. As with the urine, he had slept right through his wash so she had left him under the warm lights of the incubator. He had to be naked, the midwife had said, so that the majority of his jaundiced skin was exposed to the phototherapy. Judging by how contented he looked at the moment, Marcel didn't seem to mind having no clothes on. Sitting back on the hospital bed, Jennie fought the urge to drift off to sleep, she knew it wasn't worth the few minutes she would get. As she faded in and out of wakefulness Jennie could see Marcel was now sucking his tongue. With dewy eyed, new mum bias, she was immediately distracted from her overwhelming exhaustion by watching the sweetest action she had ever seen a baby do. She knew he'd be awake soon. The tongue sucking would soon develop into an urge for something warm and filling.

Smiling brilliantly at the health care assistant that answered her room buzzer, she asked for a cup of strong coffee and her sterilised breast pump. Jennie's nipples were sore and had scabs on them from Marcel's frantic and seemingly constant suckling. The breast pump helped to numb her nipples before she latched him on and also gave him something a bit easier to get a hold of as his mouth was so small and her boobs were huge at the moment. The milk that she expressed off was stored in the fridge and had come in handy for giving Marcel a bottle feed when she'd been home this evening and unable to feed him herself. She could sense that the person she secretly called Grumpy Grace was about to refuse, expecting Jennie to get the equipment herself, when Marcel with unusually impeccable timing, woke with his usual fanfare of screaming. Jennie leapt into action, murmuring soothing words which must have been impossible for him to hear over the volume of his shrieks. Grumpy Grace rushed off to get the requested items before Jennie could ask for help quieting Marcel.

'Thank you Marcel. We make a good team don't we sweetie?'

Jennie propped him up on her shoulder and breathed in his baby smell. Love blossomed warmly in her belly. Jennie looked despairingly at the window blind which was leaking a bit of weak daylight. *Goodbye sleep time*, she thought.

A few hours later, Marcel was still awake, wide eyed because he had a tummy ache and wouldn't settle either in the incubator or in Jennie's arms. Wearily she thought, *I am so selfish! All I really want to lie down and sleep. I'm tired of trying to give Marcel what he wants.* Tired beyond any hope of rational thought, Jennie's eyes stung with exhaustion and unshed tears. *Why wasn't Stephen answering his phone?* She was sure that she'd looked a right fool in front of the police. *What kind of a wife am I if I don't even know how to contact my husband in an emergency?* PC Stowerby had given Jennie her card and asked if she would tell Stephen to contact her when he surfaced. Jennie heaved a shuddering sigh just as a midwife came in to do her daily check. Seeing Jennie's distress she sat down and gave her a hug instead.

'Why don't I pop Marcel into his small cot and take him to the kitchen with me while I make you some sweet tea and some buttered toast? A little while out of the incubator will be ok now because his last test showed that his jaundice levels are dropping. Is there anything else I can do to help? Do you need any painkillers? Is it the break-in that's got you so upset? Would it help to talk about whatever's bothering you?'

Jennie could only shake her head or nod in the appropriate places but it was enough for the midwife to tuck Marcel in his cot and wheel him out, shutting the door quietly behind her. In the ensuing silence, Jennie could feel the relief wash over her. After bringing her the tea and toast as promised, the midwife offered to take Marcel to the nursery and do his check there so Jennie could have the time to eat in peace. Jennie again could only nod her approval, too numb with tiredness and gratitude to muster up the strength to speak. As she swallowed the last bite, she felt her tea burn her leg; she had started to drift off to sleep still holding the cup. Putting the cup down, she slid under her covers, eyes already closed as her head landed on the crackly plastic cover of the pillow. She woke with a start to find the room bathed in the glow of the incubator lights, her son sleeping deeply and a note taped to the side of the Perspex window. The note read:

I hope you had a good sleep; you looked so peaceful I didn't have the heart to wake you.

Jennie looked at her son, who was contentedly fast asleep. Instead of enjoying the sight she began fretting. *I don't understand why the midwife was able to settle Marcel when I couldn't. She must think I am a failure for falling asleep. I hope it didn't make her think that I wasn't worried about Marcel's safety.* Jennie's heart began to pound hard and fast, pulsing heat in waves up the sides of her face. *Maybe Marcel can tell that I don't know what I'm doing. Maybe he doesn't love me, that is possible isn't it? For a baby to not bond with his mother?* The immensity of those thoughts sucked at her, dragging her towards a space in her head that felt very scary and out of control. Jennie didn't want to go there and began thinking very hard about not thinking those kinds of thoughts. Her efforts were partially successful with her mind just sort of skidding around the edges of the fears and then skittering away before it could get caught by them. Up till this point she had been grateful for the hospital's strict partners only visiting policy but now she wondered if this was a bit excessive for someone like her who had to stay in several days. She could have done with some face-to-face company from one of her friends or work colleagues. Besides Sue, she didn't really have anyone she could call a close friend anymore as she had been so wrapped up in her pregnancy and relationship with Stephen and Sue wasn't the slightest bit interested in babies. Jennie's mum lived in Canada and so that support system was almost non-existent too as due to the expense, Jennie had only been able to enjoy a couple of phone calls with her on her mobile during her stay in hospital. Marcel's premature arrival meant she would have to wait even longer before her mum came. *I'm a mummy missing her mummy,* Jennie thought, feeling sad and giggly at the same time.

Seven

A few days later Jennie was feeling jubilant because Marcel's jaundice levels had stabilised at a safe level. He was allowed out of the incubator and there was even some midwifery mutterings about the possibility that they might even be able to go home later that afternoon. Jennie loved seeing Marcel in his cot instead of having to look at him through the incubator's plastic barrier. She realised that she was crying again and felt grateful that Marcel was sleeping in case her quiet sobbing scared him. She was grateful Stephen was home for a day or two, even though he had thoughtlessly invited their friends, Simon and Sue round the following evening. Jennie protested when she heard, exhausted beyond belief and wanting to be alone enjoying family time rather than entertaining guests. Simon and Sue were notorious for not leaving until no one else was standing.

'Perhaps I can use toothpicks to prop my eyelids open... nope bad idea, they'd never leave.'

'Ah Jennie, it's just a bit of fun, you need to lighten up a bit,' Stephen slid his upper and bottom lip in opposite directions to each other, an expression which, in the past, had never failed to make her laugh.

A tearful giggle which sounded somewhat like a hysterical half hiccup, escaped from behind Jennie's lips which, until that moment, had been pressed tightly together. She had hoped that Stephen would have lost his urge to party after she had been unable to get a hold of him when they were burgled. Stephen claimed to have been horrified when he got her phone message the following day and he'd apologised profusely for not letting her know he was out clubbing.

'A quiet beer at the pub to celebrate Marcel's arrival grew into an unplanned, full on night out, darling. I was so exhausted from Marcel's birth that I got sloshed really quickly. Then I dropped my phone in a puddle and it wouldn't work till I had dried it out overnight.' His eyes were widely innocent, the tone of his voice soft and loving.

Jennie felt herself falling for his excuse, or perhaps it was seeing a soft look in his eyes for the first time in a while that made her drop the line of questioning.

Jennie got up and walked over to gaze at Marcel lying spread eagle and fast asleep in his cot. He looked adorable dressed in clothes instead of the sleepwear she had dressed him in when he had come out of the incubator for feeds. Teensy, blue jeans made of amazingly soft denim, a long sleeved tee shirt and fluffy striped socks, all made in premature baby sizes. Stephen had gone to the parent and baby superstore for premature baby sized nappies and sleep suits and ended up buying several day wear outfits from their premature baby range. They had everything, Stephen had said, from socks to hats. Jennie, who had no idea such things existed marvelled at the cleverness of the designer who created the clothing range. She smiled at her six day old sleeping son, her face brightening with the love that washed over her each time she looked at him and decided that she might feel better about a lot of things once they were settled in at home.

Eight

Stephen had hung banners on the front room windows. "WELCOME HOME" and "A BABY BOY" they declared to all those who passed by. It was a cheery sight to be welcomed with as they pulled up in front of the house. She felt proud of what they had achieved and glad Stephen was inclined to declare his joy to the neighbourhood.

'Just making sure everyone knows my boy is home,' said Stephen in response to Jennie's delight.

Oh so he isn't welcoming me home, is that what he is trying to imply? Jennie's face fell in response to the downward mood swing that thought caused and the day suddenly seemed a little less bright. At least Stephen had made a start on clearing up the mess left by the robbers. The graffiti was still on the walls but it was now faint and illegible. The shelves in their front room which had once housed their TV, DVD player, stereo and speakers were empty except for some flowers and a box of chocolates.

Jennie went over for a closer look at the flowers which turned out to be a potted mix of chrysanthemums and a tiny tea rose. The chocolates were all dark, her favourite. Her heart lifted, 'Oh Stephen, how sweet, thank you.'

'They're from Sue, she dropped them round this morning on her way to work. I've had a go at sorting the mess down here and in our room but Marcel's room is still in a right state. I've been shattered what with the cleaning and running back and forth to the General to see you both and thought that seeing as he'll be in with us for a while it doesn't matter about his room for now.'

A few hours after they arrived home, Jennie realised that Marcel wouldn't settle for more than an hour unless he was snuggled up against her chest in his sling. Jennie fast became an expert in doing most things while wearing the sling on this first day at home, including going to the toilet which reminded her of the physical awkwardness she had willingly endured during pregnancy.

When she had finally managed to force herself to go and

look, it had made her queasy to see the window frame in Marcel's room marked with fingerprint powder. The crime team had come in the day after the burglary to dust the house for prints. They had left an information leaflet which claimed that the powder should wash off with soap and water. Well she had tried to wash it off that evening and wished she hadn't as it now looked like nicotine stains, a grim yellow reminder of the vile event.

She was glad that Marcel wouldn't be in there on his own for a long time as she wouldn't feel safe leaving him in a room that was easily broken into. Though deep down, somewhere cynical inside her, she was certain that any kidnapper would soon bring him back when Marcel started one of his marathon crying jags. Jennie shook her head in an attempt to shed her frustration as she thought, *this boy of mine could cry for England; in fact he's an Olympian stridently lusty wailer.*

'Stephen, I can't get these damn marks off. I wish you'd tried to get rid of them straight after they'd finished!'

'I wasn't here woman. I was working!' he said in an ominously quiet voice.

Guilt flooded her as she realised that she'd snapped at Stephen and in front of Marcel too. What kind of a mum was she anyway? Once again she reprimanded herself for forgetting that Stephen was finding the responsibility of fatherhood stressful too and his personality change was just his way of dealing with it, she hoped. Now that she was home she intended to make every effort to be a more calm and understanding wife. To take the time to get to know her husband inside and out.

Why did I think it was a good idea to marry a man I knew so very little about? Since seeing the gloomy and occasionally less than kind side to Stephen's personality Jennie was beginning to regret her hasty decision. To give Stephen credit where it was due, he did seem to genuinely adore Marcel, Jennie reminded herself. *Shame those emotions don't appear to extend to being willing to make an effort to moderate what he says to me,* Jennie felt her chest tighten as she drifted through this last thought. *Marry in haste and repent at leisure.* Jennie sighed. She could remember the grandmother she was named after, Jennie, not Jenny and never Jennifer, using the "marry in haste" saying in reference to someone's suspiciously hasty and apparently unwise matrimonial when she was a young child. *You might be right Grammie*, Jennie thought, *but I am going to do my best to prove you wrong.*

Nine

The day after they arrived home from hospital, Donna the midwife came to do Jennie and Marcel's postnatal check.

'What a clever boy you are Marcel! You are doing everything just right and the jaundice should clear in its own time,' she smiled a "well done" look in Jennie's direction.

'I am still worried that he doesn't look at me before, during or even after a feed though,' Jennie forced this out and braced herself for Donna's response.

'Oh give the poor premature boy a chance! You'll be expecting him to walk before he's weaned,' Donna chided Jennie.

Best keep my mouth shut and be grateful he is healthy, Jennie berated herself.

'Let's see how Marcel gets on over the next couple of weeks and if this jaundice hasn't started fading you can take him to the doctor's for a blood test to see if there is anything else going on,' Donna suggested, assuming wrongly that Jennie's main concern was Marcel's jaundice.

Jennie nodded absentmindedly; as soon as Donna had rejected her concerns about Marcel, she had stopped concentrating on what she was saying. Instead she was worrying about getting the house, herself and Marcel ready for Simon and Sue's visit. Simon and Sue, the mutual friends who had introduced them, were due round at 6pm, thanks to Stephen inviting them for supper. She was less than happy that their visit was being extended beyond the original "cup of tea" scenario.

'What's your problem? Loosen up woman! I don't understand how you can keep moaning about being tired. You've done nothing all morning but laze around the house with Marcel attached to your tit or sleeping in the sling! We'll get a takeaway for fuck's sake! All you have to do is entertain our friends. I've got a few days off work and have every right to want to enjoy myself on my days off,' Stephen had blustered all this in her direction without taking his eyes off the football match on the telly the evening before. No point trying to explain, yet again, how exhausting it was to care for a demanding baby, get the house as spotless as it was before the burglary and be bright and sparkling, while delivering witty small talk to friends who rarely and unconvincingly offered to help with anything, Jennie thought grimly. Instead she just let him verbally strut around displaying his tail feathers like an overly confident peacock.

'Well I'd better get moving through the rest of these postnatal checks, Sue's gone off with a bad back again so we are a bit short staffed, for a change!' Donna, ever the un-professional when it came to work gossip, laughed cynically and startled Jennie out of her reverie.

'Oh sorry Donna, I was miles away. I am finding it a shock to be home without the buzzer close by when I feel I need help. Also it was nice to not have to clean or tidy when I was in the maternity unit. Being home is more of a struggle than a pleasure right now,' she said as she got up to see Donna to the door.

'Well it is early days yet, you've been home less than forty eight hours. Why don't you let Stephen take over for you tonight? He could give Marcel your expressed milk in a bottle for a few feeds so you can have some time to yourself!' She flung one last smile in Jennie's direction and walked down the pavement to her car.

Great idea but wrong man, thought Jennie sadly. Stephen would be far too busy drinking himself stupid with Simon and Sue tonight and he seemed to view basic baby care as a woman's job.

That afternoon they were going on their first outing. Marcel needed more nappies, Jennie and Stephen were shocked at the amount he went through. How could someone so small produce so much waste? Stephen had insisted on carrying Marcel while Jennie was in charge of the empty pushchair. They'd use it to cart the nappies home and Jennie would need it if Marcel woke for a feed while they were out. It was easier to pop him in the pushchair and whizz off to a feeding area than to mess about transferring the sling from Stephen to her. Stephen strode proudly along the precinct, looking every inch the perfect father with his tiny son snug in the sling. Carrying Marcel made him feel useful and meant he could enjoy by proxy the attention lavished on Marcel from fellow shoppers.

'Oh isn't he a tiny poppet! He's a lucky boy to have his daddy carry him round!' said one tiny old woman before directing the next comment at Jennie, 'You are blessed to have such a willing husband! Mine never lifted a finger to help me with ours; mind you things were different in our day.' Her voice quavered and wobbled, as ancient as the body it came from.

You don't know the half of it old woman, Stephen thought but sensibly kept to himself. 'My little man is a whole nine days old today!' Stephen beamed at his new ally.

Jennie, who found it very odd that complete strangers would stop to comment on the behaviour of a family they did not know; could only smile weakly at the pair of them. She was overwhelmed with exhaustion. Marcel might be nine days old today but she had spent the first six days in hospital and had yet to build up her strength. Marcel's birth had left her physically deplete and the ensuing sleep deprived days had further depleted her emotionally. Jennie prayed silently that the opinionated old woman would stop talking and let them finish up and get home before Marcel woke up. Inevitably, the wailing started, and Marcel was swiftly solely her labour of love once again. Stephen took the opportunity to vanish into various boy toy gadgets shops.

'Text me when you've got him sorted and we'll carry on,' his tone of voice indicating he felt he was indulging her in a little whim by leaving Jennie to sit on the bench in a smelly nappy changing area while she breastfed Marcel. Jennie looked around as Marcel guzzled his meal, she couldn't believe this was what was offered to parents looking to feed their babies when out shopping, it was the equivalent to an adult being served a meal in a toilet. Marcel didn't' seem to care though; he was too busy making loud glugging noises as he greedily fed from both breasts, fists clenched and eyes squeezed shut. Instead of enjoying their closeness during the

51

feed, Jennie stared at the wall and worried. The house was still not cleaned to her satisfaction and she would have liked a nap before Simon and Sue arrived. *What if they stay well past any hope of me being able to catch up on the lost sleep? What if I fall asleep when I'm supposed to be enjoying their company? Why doesn't Stephen feel as exhausted as I do?* Jennie felt herself drifting off to sleep on the wake of these worries and pinched her leg hard in order to wake herself up fully. Chivalry was certainly dead in their house. In fact it seemed that Stephen was starting to snap at her for the slightest thing lately. Earlier he'd called her a nagging harpy when she'd suggested they pop into the police station on their way home from the shops, as Stephen had still not been in to leave his fingerprints. She'd given hers' on the night of the burglary for elimination purposes and PC Stowerby had asked if Stephen would come in at his convenience to do the same.

I was only trying to be helpful, why does he have to take it the wrong way every time? Jennie wondered, the wall in front of her growing increasingly blurry as she fought to keep her tears from spilling.

Ten

As Jennie had predicted, Simon and Sue had stayed late, long past the end of the cup of tea and Turkish takeaway she'd suggested, in the hopes that they leave earlier if they had no chance to consume any alcohol. No such luck. The cork was being pulled out of the first bottle of red before she'd finished washing up their supper stuff. Simon and Stephen, intent on rehashing old times, had paid little attention to Jennie or Marcel all evening. Jennie hadn't minded being ignored by Stephen. She'd come to feel a bit twitchy over the last few months, when his eyes fell on her with that questioning intensity that always seemed to find her lacking in any category he happened to choose. Sue, in her well-rehearsed "sweet little girl" fashion (which never failed to set Jennie's teeth on edge) had clung to Simon's hand or arm, looking up at his face and asked leading questions all evening. The men had responded well to this tactic which gave them ample opportunity to paint themselves in the most favourable light.

Jennie had sat silently enjoying Marcel's warmth and wondering when Sue, who she knew to be incredibly intelligent, would stop pretending to be a vacant blonde. All evening she had waited for everyone else to notice and comment on Marcel's good behaviour. *Sue hadn't even asked to hold him and how could anyone resist?* Jennie wondered, forgetting that she too, had once been underwhelmed by babies. Not being able to drink alcohol and therefore finding it hard to enjoy the drunken inanity, Jennie had said goodnight and made her way to bed. She knew Marcel would wake her many times before morning. Best to be sensible, the lack of sleep in the days since his birth were starting to make her feel jetlagged. As she lay down she could hear another wine cork being pulled from its bottle. Following the pop, came the sound of Stephen apologizing to Simon and Sue for Jennie's rudeness in going up to bed while they were still there.

Sue giggled, pointlessly as far as Jennie could tell, and

Simon said, 'Neva mind pal, her loss and our gain! Let's get stuck into that bottle and she'll soon be able to hear what a good time she's missin!'

Jennie felt tears run hotly down her cheek, slide warmly past her ear and splash onto her pillow. Why didn't Sue come to her defence? She was supposed to be her friend.

That next morning Jennie had woken feeling absolutely dreadful. Marcel was still sleeping but she simply could not. Stephen's snoring and farting was not conducive to a restful atmosphere for overtired mums. She'd learnt by now not to complain about Stephen's obnoxious farting as he always responded with "Better out than in!" Resentfully, she realised that she was still smarting from the emotional injuries she'd sustained on their trip to town yesterday. Jennie decided to try and cheer up as Stephen was going away again for work in less than forty eight hours. She didn't want him to leave on a bad note and decided it would be better to push her feelings aside so they could make the most of indulging in the luxury of this time together to hone their new parenting skills. She slid her legs out from under the covers and swung them over the side of their bed. Stephen twitched and farted. Jennie walked over to the window and opened it wide, leaving the curtains open just a little so some watery early morning sunlight streamed in but not enough to wake Marcel who was still asleep in his Moses basket. Stephen's grunt had a question mark at the end.

'Morning! Cuppa?' Jennie whispered with false cheer.

'Please, ta.' Stephen mumbled with a mouth that sounded dry.

Jennie made two cups of tea, milk and honey for her and stewed with two sugars for Stephen and brought them back upstairs. She placed a cup on each of their bedside tables and slid back under the covers and sat propped up on pillows against the headboard. Stephen did the same and they sat, sipping tea in peaceful silence for a few moments until Marcel squeaked in his sleep. Soon after he began sucking his tongue and flailing his arms. Stephen and Jennie sighed simultaneously then looked at each other and grinned.

'Soon be bath time. Help me?' Jennie asked, handing this as an olive branch to Stephen. Bath time was her favourite time with Marcel and Stephen knew it.

'Bit scared I'll drop him, truth be told. You hold him and I'll wash?'

'Sure! Sounds like fun. I'll just give him his feed and then we'll get him sorted. He'll love having both of us making a fuss over him at the same time.' *And, I'll love it too* Jennie thought.

That day passed in a haze of parental bliss and by the time Stephen left for work the next evening Jennie had managed to convince herself that they had called a truce on whatever unspoken problems had been disrupting their relationship. Little did she know that Stephen's work related absences went a long way towards compounding their relationship difficulties. Stephen was going away for just over two weeks this time, a week of 'team building' in the Norfolk Broads and then a week working in Italy.

While Stephen was gone Jennie slipped into a cozy blur of daily routine. She always woke thirsty, so Jennie would sneak in a cup of tea before Marcel's morning feed. Feeding Marcel in bed in the morning was the greatest feeling, all snuggly and warm, followed by his bath and another feed. Then while he dozed fitfully in his bouncy chair in the bathroom, she'd shower and get dressed and eat a quick breakfast. Then after another feed for Marcel, usually a short one which Jennie thought of as his 'drink', she'd pop him in his sling to keep him settled and do some housework or walk to the midwifery postnatal clinic at Titchfield General's community midwifery centre. Marcel was still jaundiced but the midwives reassured her that this should start fading as he got older. Every afternoon, depending on the weather, Jennie would walk or drive to the shops to get enough food for herself and a treat or toy for Loopy the cat. He was adjusting slowly to Marcel and Jennie felt the treats helped make her feel better about having less attention for Loopy though she had to admit they didn't exactly have the same affect on Loopy. Sure he'd scoff the treats and indulge her by playing half heartedly with the toys but he still tried to squeeze onto her lap each time she sat down to feed Marcel. Marcel didn't seem to mind Loopy's presence during feeds so they reached a compromise of sorts, with Marcel propped up on Loopy instead of a pillow during feeds. *Unusual, a bit strange and probably not everyone's concept of a good idea but hey it works* Jennie thought as she settled her cat and son on her lap for the afternoon feed. The afternoon feeds tended to be long ones and Jennie would smooth Loopy's fur as Marcel fed and relaxed lulled by the feel of Loopy's purrs. Marcel could be relied upon to sleep for at least two solid hours in the afternoon and Jennie always slept during this time too unless she was expecting a call from Stephen. In the evenings Jennie would Skype her mum or chat on the phone, if Marcel was settled enough, to Sue and the occasional work colleague who called. These conversations were invariably strained as Jennie had nothing she wanted to talk about besides Marcel and only her mum was as interested in that subject as she was.

Eleven

'I've joined a "Sure Start" breastfeeding group that meets weekly for lunch; it's great to have people to chat with. Also it's nice to see that all the other mums with four week old babies look as awful as I do. We've decided to put up a poster on the door that says, "No Yummy Mummies allowed!"' Jennie grinned down the phone to her mum. They had been on the phone for the better part of an hour while Marcel, tired out from the afternoon's long walk home, slept in his pushchair. Jennie sometimes wondered why she'd ever invested in a Moses basket as the three wheeler pushchair with its leg cosy functioned more than adequately as a bed when the seat was fully reclined.

'Glad to hear you've found some people to share your time with. I think it is such a shame none of your friends have young babies and was starting to get worried that you would find it lonely being a new mum. Is Marcel enjoying the outings too? Are you happy darling? Oh I wish I didn't live so far away.'

'Dunno if Marcel is enjoying himself mum, it's so hard to tell with him. He seems to be the only baby who doesn't settle after eating; in fact he isn't even really settled during feeds. I wish you lived closer too mum. I know you like the sunshine and lifestyle you get in the Okanagan but I wish you'd moved somewhere on the Mediterranean instead of all the way to Canada.' Jennie's grin disappeared as she deliberately avoided the question about whether she was happy or not. After saying goodbye to her mum, she stood with her back against the corridor wall. The ugly nubby wood chip paper was irritating but she felt too agitated to sit down and too tired to stay upright without support.

Jennie's mind drifted back to the sight of all those other babies gazing adoringly at their mums, their bodies curled round in a classic feeding baby style cuddle. A flashback to the intense feelings of jealousy resurfaced. Unable to watch the others any longer, she had concentrated on Marcel's long eyelashes. *He'll probably hate them when he gets older, more's the shame*, Jennie thought. Beautiful they were and she had told Stephen, in no uncertain terms, that he had better get those thoughts of trimming them down to a more "manly" length out of his head. He was growing eyebrows now and the hair on his ears had finally fallen out, unlike the load of hair on his back, she had often wondered where he got that gene from.

All in all, she had enjoyed the group; it was nice to have snacks to pick at, ready laid out on the table and someone making her cups of tea. However, every time someone had wandered over and started talking to her, Marcel had twitched and whimpered or came off her breast and started crying. Jennie wondered if she tensed up when she had a conversation. She wasn't social by nature, small talk didn't come naturally to her and she couldn't imagine why else Marcel would react like that when he should be totally engrossed in feeding. There had been a health visitor present at the last group and she had agreed that Marcel did act differently from the other babies there but Jennie couldn't seem to make her grasp the fact that this wasn't a one off for Marcel, that the behaviours had been firmly established from a few days after his birth. The health visitor said that perhaps being born prematurely had made him a bit anxious.

'I expect he will begin to settle down as he gets a bit older. If he doesn't then make sure you tell the health visitor who is linked to your GP's surgery of your concerns to get the ball rolling.'

"What ball and rolling where?" was what Jennie wanted to know but she felt too embarrassed to ask. At least now she knew it wasn't just her imagination telling her that Marcel behaved differently from other children his age. Somehow this made her feel better and utterly devastated at the same time. Jennie was grateful that her mum would be with her in a couple of months. She needed her support and an opinion about her mothering skills from someone she trusted.

One of the many great things to anticipate in regards to her mum's visit was that it would mean that Stephen would be forced to resume sleeping in their bed. He had taken to sleeping in the spare room lately; claiming he was beginning to suffer from Marcel's constant waking. Jennie had a sense that he wasn't telling the whole truth for wanting to sleep in the spare room but couldn't imagine what ulterior motive he could have. Perhaps all new dads felt and behaved like he was, she'd love to ask some of the women in her postnatal group but couldn't bring herself to raise the subject for fear of finding out that her situation was indeed unique. In fact, Stephen seemed to have lost all desire for her since she got pregnant, when she'd questioned this; he had said he was scared of hurting their baby. Perhaps she'd ask her mum about his odd urges to sleep alone and his zero libido during her visit or perhaps not. Maybe that kind of stuff was best discussed with Sue; at least she liked Stephen and wouldn't automatically assume the worst in relation to his behaviour.

Jennie watched Marcel fidgeting around in his sleep; he was in constant motion, her baby, it was a wonder he didn't sleep more deeply. *Why doesn't he wear himself out? Maybe the lack of restful sleep is why he is always such a cross patch.* Stephen had claimed it was nothing to do with the lack of sleep and that Marcel simply got his personality from Jennie. Jennie didn't think she was coping too badly on a few hours sleep each day, okay maybe she was a bit weepy but she hadn't thought she was coming across as a grumpy cow. She flinched as a hazy memory from the middle of the night surfaced. She had almost dropped Marcel the night before while feeding him in the rocking chair. Breastfeeding was a delight now and it was hard to believe it would ever be so simple and enjoyable after the pain she'd experienced in the first week but with the pleasure came the waves of relaxation increasing her urge to succumb to the lure of sleep. Horror flashed through her as she relived the panicky realisation that her arms had dropped and Marcel had been slipping out of them. That had woken her in a hurry and then she couldn't get back to sleep after Marcel was settled in his Moses basket. Every time she drifted off she had imagined she could feel him slipping out of her arms again and would jolt wake with her heart pounding. Sensibly, Jennie decided to take the opportunity to curl up on the couch and indulge in a nap until Marcel fidgeted himself awake in his pushchair.

Twelve

Marcel had been difficult all day, only drifting off to sleep a few minutes before Stephen swaggered in. Although it was Valentine's Day, Jennie hadn't been foolish enough to expect flowers, chocolates or any other material token of affection but a kind word would have done wonders to lift her spirits. What had happened to their happy bubble, surely she hadn't imagined it all? When she felt rested enough, hopefully sometime before Marcel began walking, she planned to try and talk to Stephen about his belittling behaviour.

Stephen caught Jennie drifting off in the armchair with Marcel still in the sling and spat, 'Had an easy day lounging around while some of us are out slogging our guts out at work I see. What's that delicious smell? Let me guess... a steak grilled just the way I like it with all the trimmings? No? What a surprise! Don't suppose you've bothered to get Marcel off your tit long enough to even make me some food have you? That's the thanks I get for all my hard work is it?' The scorn on his face scorched its way to her eyes, blinding her to any hope of a pleasant evening. What Jennie couldn't know was that the scorn on his face hid the gloom and loneliness that welled up inside him, the abyss that even the love he felt for his son couldn't help him bridge. Someday soon he knew he was going to have to make a decision one way or the other.

Jennie sighed and started to slide off the chair to go start supper, she imagined that she could feel her very bones aching with tiredness but that could be ignored, unlike his tirade. Why had she never noticed this side of him before Marcel was born? Jennie wondered.

'No! Don't change a habit of a lifetime,' Stephen sneered, conveniently forgetting that Jennie's pre-Marcel hobby had been to cook up gourmet meals. It had helped put her into what her mother would have termed a "Zen state" after spending the day force-feeding children the education they would rather not absorb. The fact that those poor kids had a lot to contend with did much to soften her disposition towards their challenging classroom behaviours. Challenging or not, Jennie loved teaching primary school children and those children in particular had brought out her mothering instinct. Jennie had prided herself with creating a stimulating learning environment for them that reached beyond their social barriers. She also brought in homemade cookies on a regular basis into which she had added grated carrot or apple to the chocolate laced batter in an attempt to add some nutrients into their diet as well as a little token of kindness into their daily lives. Now that she had a child of her own she wondered if she would be able to keep up the demanding pace of nurturing the deprived children in her classroom and then having enough energy leftover to lavish her full attention on Marcel on she got home. More than once since Marcel's arrival Jennie had considered that she may need to find a job that was less emotionally draining.

Most of the children in her class lived on the Barnstead Avenue Estate. It was the roughest council estate in a city which had more than its fair share of estates scoring high on the National multiple deprivation charts. Those children had a lot to contend with, cramped housing with inadequate heating, too thin walls which made them privy to all they didn't yet need to know about the effects of substance abuse, domestic violence and other disturbing aspects of their reality. They often came into school suffering the after effects of too little sleep and too much neglect. The fall out usually surfaced around 10 am when the sugar-laden breakfast wore off and exhaustion triumphed. In all fairness, Jennie knew that some of their parents did their level best to care for their children but they were battling against noisy neighbours and too little money. Before Jennie had begun her maternity leave there was a spate of cars being set alight which the children had found terribly exciting and made Jennie fear that many of them would be lured into adrenaline producing risk taking of the same ilk. Jennie had worried in the run up to her maternity leave about how the children would cope with her absence. They'd got used to her bringing them treats and had started to settle more in class although there were always challenges when they returned after half term breaks until they adjusted to the school routine again. Jennie had frequently fretted about their future. She knew that at least a small minority of them were virtually guaranteed to not grow up to be law abiding citizens, and Jennie wondered why they would bother when crime appeared so much more exhilarating than the mundane promise of working a low paying unsatisfying job. Jennie also feared that her classroom charges, the neglected kids of their neighbourhood, could see and would crave the attention crime attracted. No matter that this attention eventually earned convictions and jail time, as any love deprived child could tell you; any attention was better than none. Jennie sighed as she was wrenched from her thoughts by the sound of Stephen's voice from the front room.

'Simon and Sue are having a Valentine's party and they've invited me. They assumed that you wouldn't want to come after you fell asleep on them last time they were here.'

Jennie snorted defiantly, shook her head and clamped her lips shut on the retort which had been about to escape.

Instead she called out, 'Go Stephen... enjoy yourself, you've earned a treat after all you've been through, what with becoming a new dad and all!'

Thirteen

Valentine's day, schmalentines day! Jennie thought angrily; wide awake in the early hours of yet another day. Stephen had returned blind drunk. She had been waiting up in the front room when he arrived home. She'd already heard him vomit and fall over the dustbin so when he finally got the key in the lock she was waiting behind the door to lock it again before he had a chance to try the door handle. He was so out of it she was sure he hadn't realised what had happened. She put a wedge under the door in case he managed to get the key in again and took herself and Marcel off to bed. Taking charge of the situation in order to protect Marcel gave her a sense of power and fulfilment. *Stephen had better watch out because this is a feeling I could easily grow to crave,* Jennie thought and smiled as she drifted off to sleep, enjoying the rich tones of the doorbell and the just audible harmony of Stephen's curses.

Stephen hauled himself off to his car to sleep.

'Stupid bitch! Why didn't she come to let me in?' he complained to the night air. He thought it was outrageous that he worked hard all day while she got to sit there on maternity leave complaining she was tired and worried about Marcel. He'd talked to Simon about this and they'd decided that anyone with half a brain could see she was bored and attention seeking. That nanny show on TV said all demanding babies needed discipline in the form of a firm feeding schedule and they soon slept through the night. *He's a lovely boy, my son, and she's doing her best to make him out to be a bad 'un,* Stephen thought. Still feeling sick he leaned his head out the window and vomited again feeling surprised when the pavement moved away from the splatters.

My drink must have been spiked, he thought woozily and then heard a resonant voice murmur, 'Had a bit too much to drink? You wouldn't be planning on driving anywhere now would you?' The Community Warden grimaced in distaste looking at his soiled shoes. From experience he knew he'd have to re-wax them; vomit always stripped off the shine, right down to the leather.

'Dodgy kebab... haven't dropped a drunk all night! My lazy bitch of a wife won't get out of bed to let me out... I mean in!' Stephen slurred and stumbled through the lie in his drunken fugue.

'I don't expect anyone would want you in their house in that state and using that kind of language. Kindly step out of the car so I can run a few tests on you, you're lucky those keys weren't in the ignition or I'd be taking your licence away!' the Warden stepped aside as Stephen lunged for him.

'You pigs are all the same, wanna ruin everything a man's worked for,' he spluttered.

Stephen's alcohol laden brain was fixated on his anger with Jennie and he was determined to take it out on anything in striking distance. *By God she's hard work,* he thought. *Always expecting me to account for my whereabouts when I'm not at home and switched my phone off, the nerve of the woman after all I've had to give up because of her.* Feeling a little weepy, Stephen reassured himself, *I love my little man to bits, anyone can see that for looking, what more does she expect from me?* By the time Stephen had hauled himself upright, the reinforcements had arrived in the shape of two duty police officers who hauled Stephen off to the local cells to sleep off his excesses and regain a hold on his temper.

The next morning, in the harsh light of semi sobriety, Stephen was feeling anything but feisty. He was glad he wasn't at home, the very thought of what Marcel's crying would do to his already wounded brain made him wince. *The real thing would likely make my brains dribble out of my ears,* Stephen decided, and then winced. Thinking of Marcel caused some random thoughts to surface in the form of a forgotten task.

'Oh bollocks! I was supposed to leave my prints so some pig can pretend to be trying to catch the fuckers who'd helped themselves to the contents of my house!' Stephen thumped his forehead after his outburst and struggled to think of the name of the cop who wanted his prints through the thudding in his head. The thud of keys on his cell door somehow helped Stephen align his thoughts into an orderly fashion.

'Let's get you on your way home,' said the PC as he flung the door open and then ushered Stephen out of the cell.

Stephen followed the PC docilely down the corridor, no hint of the anger he'd felt last night remained, just his pounding head and waves of guilt for behaving so badly towards Jennie. He knew he needed to put a stop to this behaviour, knew it wasn't acceptable and knew he had to act like a man and explain to Jennie why he had been struggling with his moods these past few months. *Soon,* Stephen told himself, *I've got to get it over with soon. She knows I love Marcel and she can't take him away from me, no matter what she feels like after I've come clean to her and told her everything.* Stephen stood quietly at the discharge desk, running through opening lines he could use to broach the subject with Jennie while the PC went for his personal belongings and the discharge clerk began the necessary paperwork.

'Sign here.' The man behind the desk interrupted Stephen's flow of thought.

Stephen did so and remembered to mention his fingerprints were needed elsewhere, 'Can you pass my prints onto a PC Sowerby? She wants them on another matter, cheers matey!'

'That's PC Stowerby, you cheeky sod, watch yer'self or you'll be straight back in there,' the overworked and underpaid clerk said grimly. Stephen walked out into the soft early morning sunshine and headed to Simon's. He wasn't ready to face Jennie yet, he needed to get his thoughts in order first.

Fourteen

Stephen had massive respect for Simon who had become the closest thing he had to family for many years until Marcel was born. With a father who drank more than was good for the family dynamics and a mother so deep in denial that she thought it perfectly normal to maintain the alcohol supply in the house by regularly making copious amounts of homebrew, they were the poster family for "dysfunctional". Stephen's parents were so caught up in each other that they often forgot to parent him beyond meeting his basic needs of food, shelter and comfort. His father demanded more and more of Stephen's mother's time until Stephen felt his dad was more of a child than he. Stephen's conflicts were primarily with his father who veered from one extreme of emotion to the other. One day he could be great fun, taking Stephen on exhilarating expeditions at high speed around town on the back of his motorbike and then as soon as the very next day he might fall into a rage with Stephen for the slightest indiscretion. His mother flitted between the two of them, always trying to be the peacemaker but ultimately siding with his father. At these times Stephen would storm out of the house to hang out with friends and complain about his parents, feeling rejected, pride shrieking at the unfairness of it all once again. This parenting seesaw continued to flip flop, unsettling Stephen who could never quite relax around his father. He began to goad his dad by rebelling with increasing frequency, seeking the addictive, somewhat sickening thrill of riding his father's emotional rollercoaster. When he was seventeen Stephen threw a party one night while they were away for the weekend. His party guests, many more than were originally invited, had spread out from the kitchen and garden where Stephen had intended the party to happen and had destroyed most of the soft furnishings in the house. His father went mad when they came home and saw the damage. Stephen, hungover, scared and guilty retaliated by shouting instead of apologising and his dad decided that this was one angry teenage outburst too many

67

and told him never to come back. Stephen did come back, of course, just as he always did after he'd had time to calm down and estimated that his father had done the same but this time he found that his key didn't work in the door.

He knocked, loudly, until his dad flipped open the front room window and hissed, 'I told you to get out and I meant it. You don't like our rules so fuck off and live somewhere else!'

Stephen hadn't tried to contact his parents since that ultimate rejection. That day he went to the council's housing office and was placed in a teenage homeless shelter. He went to bed angry, cried himself quietly to sleep and woke the next morning filled with resolve to prove his parents wrong. *Not that I'm ever speaking to them again*, Stephen thought angrily. Stephen stayed at the shelter until he had completed the army recruitment process. Looking back he supposed that, subconsciously, he had been looking for a surrogate family. He'd met Simon, also a new recruit, on their first day. After they had completed the rigors of basic training, the army was the best job anyone could have, or so Stephen thought. The soldiers were never expected to think independently in any aspect of life that did not involve weapons and war tactics. Their food, laundry, washing and rest times were all scheduled in a rigid routine. The lower ranked soldiers deferred to Stephen and Simon and often did their duties in order to gain goodwill. They spent the next eight years playing soldiers during daylight hours and drinking from dusk till dawn in the skirmish free zones they were posted to.

Stephen had found the realities of life after discharge from service a harsh shock, nothing came easily and he felt that he had earned the right to be indulged by society. Follow orders and everything else will fall into place for you, that was what he'd been taught during those eight years. Stephen and Simon quickly fell back into their routine of working the minimum amount they could and then partying hard until the early hours of the morning. With no one imposing the strict daylight routine on them, they began to routinely oversleep.

In a matter of months, they both lost enough jobs that they virtually rendered themselves unemployable. Petty crime was a very short step away from the place they now found themselves in and the allure of easy money was irresistible. However, they found themselves to be rather unskilled at this as well. Simon got caught first and in short order was sent off to jail.

Stephen, bored without his mate, began to drink heavily. His life pretty much deteriorated without Simon, his buddy, his bruv. The alcohol, which he bought in increasing quantities, compliments of his dole cheque, meant that he also ate less and less in order for his money to stretch to more alcohol. That had the added benefit of preventing him from turning into a "fat knacker" he had consoled himself. Stephen knew he was fighting a losing game; the money he got from the government each week wasn't enough to fund his increasing capacity for alcohol. Eventually he realised he needed to get a job. He managed to con someone into letting him drive their unlicensed mini-cab during the day. Due to start on Monday, he celebrated his future cash flow by drinking on tab at the pub most of Sunday afternoon and evening, promising to return with his day's earnings the very next evening.

He was drunk enough to stumble several times on the short walk home from the pub to his bedsit but sober enough to remember to set his alarm and also set the TV to come on loud at 7am. He woke with a start when the alarms went off, drank several cups of strong coffee and set off for work feeling very tired but not, to his astonishment, hungover. His liver had been coaxed into accepting prodigious amounts of alcohol and processing it without too many ill effects. What Stephen didn't know was that his liver could only process the alcohol at a standard rate no matter how much practice he gave it over the years and he was well over the limit as he got behind the wheel of the car that morning.

Stephen drove a few early morning fares around the city, cursing the building traffic which meant he could only creep along behind the other cars in the queue. He was awake and wanted to drive at a steady clip which would allow him to get as many fares as possible during his shift rather than waste time crawling along with the same fare for half an hour at a time. He knew it would take him all day to pay off his tab from last night at this rate and he wanted to earn enough to fund a good session that night. Much to his delight, the next fare wanted him to take her to a neighbouring city, allowing his car to get onto the motorway and let off some steam. She was a chatty girl and they were soon laughing and bantering as Stephen pushed the car into the fast lane and floored the accelerator until the needle was touching ninety. Neither of them noticed the van drifting across into their lane until the moment of impact.

Stephen regained consciousness as he was loaded onto the stretcher.

'Relax, relax, you've lost a lot of blood so try to stay calm and save the rest of it!' said a strangely jovial paramedic. 'Having said that we do want to take just a little more blood from you so we can find out what type you are, just in case you need a transfusion. Can you sign your consent for both?'

'Both whuh?' mumbled Stephen, confused and in pain.

'Consent for me to take your blood and consent in case you need a transfusion. I have to make you aware of the following risks of having a blood transfusion before you sign though.' The paramedic then proceeded to rattle off several sentences about what else the blood test might indicate in what sounded like a foreign language.

Stephen signed where he was indicated and then asked, 'Can someone please remove the ice pick from my brain?' before passing out again. He found out later that he had a concussion and needed fifty stitches to close the flap on his scalp. He had intended to ask how his passenger was while still at the scene of the accident but had drifted in and out of consciousness too frequently to remember if he had asked. Much to his disgust he remained conscious during the whole time they were sewing his head back together.

Shortly after Stephen's scalp was closed, he was arrested for driving while under the influence of alcohol and for dangerous driving which caused grievous bodily harm to his passenger. He began his nine month sentence just as Simon was about to be released. This was fortunate for Simon as it gave him time to finalise his conquest of Sue, a tiny blonde with big curves in all the right places whom he'd met as a pen pal in prison. Sue, recently widowed and already tired of the pub and club scene, had written to him saying she was looking for companionship. She'd attached a picture of herself and Simon nearly fell off his bed, she was almost cute in a pixie kind of way. Too much makeup and frizzy hair made her look slightly rough around the edges but beggars couldn't be choosers. He'd only signed up to the prison pen pal registry for a laugh with some of the other lads. The next thing he knew, he and Sue had spent more hours writing to each other and chatting on the phone than he had spent with his fellow inmates. He was lucky they hadn't mistaken his pre-occupation with Sue as open snobbery of their invitations to join in their unauthorized but very organized poker games.

Writing was a great tool for courting women in Simon's opinion. It gave him time to carefully phrase what he wanted to say. His conviction didn't seem to bother her, she'd giggled and said she liked a bit of a rough diamond when it came to men. Well he'd given her plenty of the companionship she'd asked for while in prison and was now looking forward to giving her something else. Simon decided that a big serving of what he called "Simon Sausage" should set both her and him to rights. He went to her large two bedroom flat when he was released from prison, intending to stay as long as she'd let him and after a few nights she seemed happy for him to share her space.

'Makes me feel safe,' she'd told him, nestling more snugly into his arms one night. He had been only half listening to her, intent as he was on the football game and lucky for him, had heard the yearning in her voice and grunted at the right time, squeezing her reassuringly.

When Stephen was released, he moved in with Simon and Sue.

'We've got the room, mate and want to give you a chance to find your feet again.'

'You sure it won't cause problems with Sue, she won't mind my intruding on your love nest?'

'Sue minds if I tell her to,' Simon had laughed.

'Good one pal!' Stephen wished he could think of plays on words like that.

Stephen spent a year drifting from one job to another. He was often out of town on what he claimed was "business", the nature of which he at first refused to disclose to either Simon or Sue. Once he was allowed his driving licence back, everything appeared to click into place for Stephen, much to Simon and Sue's relief.

'They don't have a problem with your driving conviction?' Simon had asked, incredulously.

'Nah man. I'm not driving for them so what's it matter, they know I've served my time.'

Stephen had landed the job as a jack man with the Toraldo Company and began to spend a lot of time touring to the various races with the cars and their drivers as well as the rest of the crew that was needed to successfully win a rally.

As things were going so well for Stephen, Sue had been thinking of ways to get Stephen to move out of their house. She thought he was a nice bloke but was beginning to resent having to clean up after two men and knew that he'd never make the move without prompting, nor would Simon expect him to. After weeks of pondering she settled on an idea that might ultimately lead to him moving out and decided to run it by Simon without telling him of her end goal.

'Babe?' Sue prodded Simon who was starting to drift off to sleep.

'Huh?'

'It's nice Stephen's working 'n all?'

'Huh, huuuh…?'

'Don't 'cha think a woman 'd be the icing on the cake for 'im?'

'Yep, I do, you wanna sort it?'

'Whachu think 'bout Jennie?'

'Babe with big eyes…'

Sue laughed and gave Simon a gentle slap. 'I'll sort a double date for us, Stephen and Jennie and reckon I'd best keep you tied to my side if I've any sense!'

Sue didn't tell Jennie about Stephen's conviction. She thought Jennie wouldn't give Stephen a chance if she knew and besides, she told herself firmly, it was Stephen's business who he wanted to tell of his conviction anyway. He'd served his time and was a reformed man from what she had observed. Sue thought Stephen was hard working, sweet and had a great sense of humour to complete the package.

From the first moment Jennie laid eyes on Stephen, the spark was there for her. Stephen, bewildered as to how the date had come about had to admit that he found Jennie's demure manner (making an unexpected appearance due to first date nerves) and huge childlike eyes, a gorgeous combination. Jennie found his boyish charm and apparently irreverent take on life, refreshing and alluring. The date turned into a very long night of drunkenness and the result of that uninhibited lust was a piece of history that came to be named Marcel. Like so many other children he was unplanned but very much loved and like so many others in his parents' situation, one of them was in the relationship under self-imposed duress.

Fifteen

Marcel's skin was still a tinge yellow. The health visitor said that as he had been jaundiced for the two months since his birth, Jennie had to take him to the doctor to have another blood test to check his liver function. Even though the health visitor said that it was a precaution only and that Marcel was likely slow to stop being yellow just because of his prematurity, Jennie still felt like crying. Not just because there might be something wrong with Marcel but also because she couldn't bear the thought of Marcel having yet another needle shoved into his heel. He was obviously traumatised by all the ones he'd endured already as he didn't even like her smoothing his feet with her fingers during the baby massage lessons. Jennie mustered up her courage and after reminding herself to act like the adult, she popped Marcel in the sling and left for the doctor's. She had such mixed feelings about motherhood. One part of her desperately didn't want to be the one who always took Marcel for checkups, blood tests and the like in case he associated her with these painful processes. The other part of her insisted she would never be able to bear not being there to try and comfort him when these things were happening to him.

The walk to the surgery calmed her. It was a lovely day and the air smelt fresh after a night of pouring rain. The cherry trees were in blossom already, softly pink and seemingly hung in the air like mist caught by the sun's rise. On the other trees, Jennie could see the first buds were starting to open in a complimentary pale green and although the snowdrops and crocuses had finished, the daffodils were still scattered in cheery swathes under the trees in the churchyard that she used as a short cut. She stopped to smell a hedge which was covered in tiny white flowers and regretted it. *How could something so pretty smell like tom cat piss?* For some reason this incongruence tickled her enough to make her giggle out loud and she walked the rest of the way to the doctor's with the pleasant sensation of a

74

small smile playing on her lips.

The doctor examined Marcel with cold instruments and even colder clinical detachment, which upset him so much that he cried till he was sick. He was silent and watchful afterwards as if the vomiting had shocked him into this unusual behaviour. The doctor wrote out the blood form and sent them to the practice nurse so she could draw the blood from Marcel. Inexplicably, Jennie started crying as soon as they crossed the threshold to the nurse's room. *Oh how embarrassing*, she thought, tears streaming silently down her cheeks.

'Hello Jennie!' said the nurse brightly as if they were old chums. 'What's with the tears? I'm not going to take the blood from you,' she chided.

'I know,' said Jennie with an embarrassingly big sniff, 'but I wish you were; I can't bear the thought of Marcel being traumatised by another blood test, he's had so many in his short life!'

'I could get quite offended by you inferring that I am going to traumatise Marcel,' said the nurse seemingly in a huff now, all traces of cheerfulness gone.

Oh shit, me and my big mouth, thought Jennie. 'No offence intended,' she said hastily. She watched as the nurse swiftly removed the necessary amount of blood, from Marcel's heel, the only sound emanating from him was the byproduct of his sucking his tongue vigorously.

'You see? All done and not a peep out of the brave boy! You new mums are all alike, working yourselves up into frenzy over nothing.'

Jennie, relieved they could leave, smiled weakly in reflexive response to the nurse's tepid smirk.

Sixteen

"Teddy Time" nursery; the name alone had made her wince but the price was right and they seemed welcoming enough on the phone, so the least she could do was go look round. Jennie discovered that there were several rooms full of bright colours and toys and the walls were adorned with the children's artwork. The noise level was at an incredible decibel but the staff were bright and affectionate with the children; sparkly voiced when speaking to them.

In hindsight Jennie was so glad she had gone, the nursery and staff seemed lovely. Marcel had behaved like an angel, fast asleep in his car seat the whole time. She giggled to herself; they sure were in for a shock when they met the real Marcel. She had booked him a place to start, on a part time trial period, two weeks before her six months worth of maternity leave ended, though whether this was to be for Marcel's benefit or hers she couldn't decide. She couldn't quite grasp the concept that she would actually have to hand Marcel over into another person's care two months from now, it seemed so wrong that new mothers had to work. Even worse somehow that she would have to hand Marcel over to be looked after by a stranger so that she could go back to work as a teacher, spending time with other people's children. Jennie reminded herself that she was lucky that as Marcel had been born early, she had no time off before his birth and had been able to make the most of spending her entire maternity leave with him. As much as she had loved every minute of her time with Marcel she had to admit that it had also been quite a full on exhausting time too. Jennie was worried she hadn't given Marcel what he needed at all times, quite terrified that he would grow to love the nursery staff more than her and fretted that he might reject her when she arrived to pick him up after work. She felt her heart clench at the very thought of losing his love.

'Oh stop being so melodramatic Jennie, children have an infinite capacity to love many people at the same time. You'll always be special to him because you are his mother,'

her own mother had told her on the phone that evening. Marcel was different though, this was what worried her, he was occasionally fretful and anxious but he didn't seem to cling to her like other babies and she was scared he wouldn't miss her when she left him at nursery. She knew that she should consider him not missing her to be a good thing and that not missing her all day could only be to his benefit.

Okay, she told herself, *time to stop thinking about it, I've got two months left as a full time mum and he might be different by then and then I'll be sad because he is missing me!* She consoled herself that she had found a nursery she trusted, with a good reputation, she felt more comfortable leaving him at a nursery instead of a child minder. In a nursery there would be everyone watching each other, a self-employed childminder couldn't offer this token of reassurance. This nursery allowed her unlimited, unannounced access too, which she found so reassuring.

Jennie grinned; having a baby sure changed her perspective on life as she now realised she was looking forward to going back to work so she could have a rest. *Still no rest for another couple of months that's for sure,* Jennie thought wryly as Marcel began to fidget and moan in his sleep, a sure sign he was waking up. She crept around getting some lunch inside herself before he woke and then bustled around making sure she had everything close at hand for his nappy change and feed as soon as he woke. Jennie turned to see him looking at her, eyes wide, from his vantage point in his high pushchair.

'HeLLO cuTie PIE!' Jennie smiled as she sang out the words. Marcel rewarded her with a sleepy half grin.

He waved his hand aimlessly in front of his face babbling nonsense until one sound stood out from the rest, 'Ma!' he declared imperiously.

'Ma? Did you say mama, baby boy?' Jennie was sure babies couldn't talk at four months old but a little encouragement could only be of benefit and she thought, who was to say Marcel wasn't a budding child prodigy?

'Ma, ma, ma, maaaaaaa!' Marcel babbled, looking over her

shoulder.

Jennie looked round feeling a bit frantic in her desire to locate the object of his interest. At last Jennie spotted it, the cat toy with a star shape at the end of a stick. It was laced with catnip and occasionally she took it away from Loopy so he'd do something other than lay on it, lick it and kick it with his feet. That morning Jennie had hung it over the raised top corner of the wooden bookcase.

'This?' Marcel's face opened into a gap jawed grin of pure delight. 'This is Loopy's! You're not a cat, you're my clever boy, oh yes you are.' Time for a diversion and Jennie knew just the thing. 'Who's a hungry boy then? You? Oh, now how did I guess that?' Jennie scooped him up and felt her milk let down at the gorgeous smell of his skin and the weight of him in her arms. Marcel hadn't shown any need for food other than her breast milk so far but that change couldn't be far off as he was feeding more frequently and for longer periods of time now. The health visitor had told her that some babies were exclusively breastfed for six months or more but Jennie was willing to bet that Marcel wouldn't be one of those babies. Once Marcel had drunk his fill and produced a couple of loud burps which were disproportionate to his size, she got out the sling. She felt her tummy wobble as she stood and sighed inwardly. She hadn't lost any of the "baby weight" she'd put on while pregnant. Scared she'd stay this plump forever she'd mentioned it to her mum the last time they'd spoken on the phone.

Laid back as usual about anything to do with motherhood Sabi had laughed and then said, 'You won't lose anything while breastfeeding sweetie. Your body had laid down stores of fat to produce plenty of good milk. It will start coming off when you wean Marcel. Until then you are not to worry about it and that is an order.'

'Okay mum, I'll try not to it's just… well the midwives, when I was pregnant, they said that breastfeeding was a good way to lose weight!'

'Well what a load of old twaddle!' Sabi snorted in derision. 'They should be ashamed of themselves for filling your head with such nonsense. Trust me your body knows what it's doing, if you are eating properly then any extra weight will go when it is the right time and it would be unhealthy to try and speed the process up! Women have had babies for millions of years and the less we mess with nature the better off we'll all be.'

'Mum! I've got two words for you... SOAP and BOX!' Jennie teased.

'That's three actually,' her mum said pedantically and then giggled.

They said their goodbyes and Jennie had hung up with a grin on her face. Everyone should be so lucky as to have a mum like hers.

Time for a walk to the library, Jennie decided after Marcel had finished feeding, with any luck he'd fall asleep and she could choose a book and a DVD or two for the week ahead. She didn't mind Stephen being away much anymore, his absences meant that she could avoid acknowledging that there were some big cracks in the surface of their relationship but it was nice to have something to fill the evenings with until her mum arrived. There was usually at least a minute or two of time to fill between settling Marcel for the first period of sleep and before she dropped like a stone into a deep sleep.

Seventeen

Satisfied that she had removed all traces of Stephen from the guest room, Jennie decided the room was ready for her mum to move into for the duration of her holiday. Stephen had not slept in their bed for a few months, not since Jennie had locked him out on Valentine's Day. He had used various excuses from Jennie banning him from the house to the excuse of Marcel constantly waking. On Sue's advice Jennie had bought Stephen some earplugs.

'Think about it Jennie, the poor man's away from home far too frequently. The last thing he wants is a bedroom full of noise. Not very welcoming is it?'

'No I suppose not but I'm quite certain that Marcel isn't really the problem, I think it is me!'

'Well you make sure you get him back in the saddle again as fast as possible. The longer you leave it the more likely he is to forget which bun his sausage belongs in!'

Jennie winced but had to acknowledge the wisdom of Sue's coarse but probably correct advice.

Stephen had refused to consider trying the ear plugs as he said the night light she used to help her see well enough to latch Marcel on for a feed would still disturb him even if he couldn't hear them moving about at night.

'It's no use Jennie, I won't be sleeping in the same bed as you no matter what clever ploy you come up with.'

Exasperation evident in her tone, Jennie said, 'Stephen, married couples are supposed to sleep in the same bed!'

'Not everyone does Jennie, show me where it says that in a rule book then, go on, show me!'

Tight lipped Jennie looked at her wedding ring, 'You used to share my bed.'

'Well I won't be going back into it Jennie, I've made up my mind!'

'How? What's to make up your mind about it? What happens when we are feeling fruity and want to do more than just sleep?' She giggled tentatively, inviting him to join her, hoping against hope that he would laugh too.

'Jennie, in case it escaped your attention, I haven't felt that way since I found out you were pregnant and now that I have seen what you went through down below I can't put that image out of my mind. I've put you on a pedestal labelled "mum". I just can't find a mum sexy. It's not you, it's me...' Seeing the distraught look on her face Stephen tried to partly make amends by saying, 'Perhaps when you've finished breastfeeding, it will be different?' Deep inside he was delighted that he had been able to find an excuse to further delay the expectation that he would want perform his marital duty.

Tears welled in Jennie's eyes, 'So you still love me then?'

Evasively Stephen said, "Course I love you numpty, you're my boy's mummy.'

The tears slipped over the brim and streaked down her cheeks as she said, 'What will I tell mum?'

'For fuck's sake woman, why would you want to discuss our sex life with your mother anyway?' Stephen stood up. 'I'm going to put the kettle on!'

'I meant, what will I tell her to explain why you're sleeping on the couch every night of her visit?' Jennie's voice was soft almost placating, as she begged his advice.

'Oh! That... well tell her that I am away with work, tell her that I am staying at Simon and Sue's so that you can have Marcel in bed with you safely, anything like that should satisfy her! Cuppa?' he said as he strode quickly from the room in his haste to be finished with this painful conversation. He knew he was treating Jennie badly and that she deserved better, the only problem was, he didn't know how to get himself out of his mess of an unwanted marriage.

Jennie bundled Marcel into his car seat and plunked a few toys on his lap along with a book for him to chew on. During the long drive to the airport Jennie amused them both by making faces and singing for Marcel who watched her every move in the rear view mirror. The face pulling caused some confusion with the boy watching her from the rear-facing seat in the people carrier in front of Jennie's car. Marcel's baby seat was so low that no one could see it from that vantage point and so he assumed that Jennie was gurning in his general direction and began making reciprocal faces. She chose to indulge the misconception as it meant that she could carry on in an attempt to satisfy her unending desire for just one more deep belly laugh from her boy. Marcel laughed himself asleep and it was only then that Jennie realized she had missed her exit by several miles and had to come off the motorway in order to trace her path back to the right junction. She pressed play on her CD player and sang along softly to the music already in there.

'Which finger did he bite? This little finger on my right,' Jennie sang the closing verse of the nursery rhyme and found herself lifting her hand off the wheel so she could wiggle the finger in question. Oh lord; she was a ruined woman without a doubt! What had happened to the person who so loved music by bands like Faithless and the like? She decided that she was lucky that she hadn't made the gesture just as she passed a man with penis size issues and resolved to try and get her habit of slipping into "mum mode" under control at least while Marcel was invisible to other people.

An hour later and hopelessly lost, Jennie pulled into a small garage for fuel and directions to the airport.

'Oh you're not far off now,' said the man at the till. 'Turn left out of here and at the next roundabout take the 3rd exit, go right at the lights, left at the ones after that and then follow the signs for Heathrow.'

Jennie mouthed the sentences to herself, looked confused and said, 'Do you have a map I could buy?'

He laughed and added it to the cost of her petrol and then marked out her route in highlighter pen after she had paid. Feeling more confident, Jennie drove off, singing loudly to placate Marcel who was by now awake and thoroughly fed up with the view from his car seat. Eventually and much to Jennie's amazement they arrived at the airport without getting lost again. Even with her detour Jennie saw that she had arrived before her mum's plane had landed and was grateful for the extra time, she fed Marcel and drank a large bottle of cool water at the same time. She was thirsty but the act of drinking also served the purpose of allowing her a convenient excuse to look away from the disapproving stares thrown her way. The stares came from people who were apparently shocked to see a woman feeding her child from the same body that had been perfectly acceptable to use as a vessel to grow him. Why breastfeeding was any different was a mystery to Jennie. Surely her body, which had produced such a marvellous miniature human being, would also know how to make a more perfect blend of milk than something generic that came in a tin? Jennie consoled herself with the knowledge that her milk was genetically specific to her baby and if strangers didn't like it then they didn't have to look.

When both of their thirsts were slaked and with all offending body parts safely stowed away, Jennie made her way to the arrivals gate with Marcel snuggled up asleep in his sling. It wasn't much of a wait till the passengers began coming through and Jennie stared hard at the doorway, looking beyond the faces as they came through to the ones behind. With a catch in her throat she shouted 'Mum!' and leapt up and down, one hand supporting Marcel in the sling, the other waving frantically to the slim grey haired woman moving her way with a huge smile on her face.

Eighteen

'Jennie I haven't seen a baby act like this since Tommy,' said her mum worriedly. Marcel had spent the past two hours screaming each time they'd dared to attempt to lie him down, as soon as they picked him up he'd settle. They'd tried walking him in his pushchair: non-stop screaming. A car ride had exactly the same result. Jennie explained that he was frequently like that and that was why she got so cross when well meaning old ladies suggested he be left to cry himself out.

'Marcel's got a mind of his own and if he wants to be cuddled then he lets me know it but other times he'll settle really well. There doesn't seem to be any reason for it either, just sometimes he is agitated for ages where nothing I do settles him except for holding him close and other times he seems quite content to be in his own space.'

'You're right sweetie, I've seen it myself now. You're not doing anything wrong. Tommy was like this!' her mum smiled gently as she said this last sentence.

Tommy was Jennie's cousin who had been non-compliant from birth. He had run his mum ragged from birth, rarely sleeping, demanding constant attention and was prone to angry outbursts if thwarted. He had spent most of his adulthood in trouble of various forms from rent arrears, unpaid speeding tickets and minor drug charges. Jennie could remember Tommy telling her that he just felt angry, all of the time, when he was sixteen years old and she was in her twenties. She was proud of the man he'd grown into, a chef who was now running his own restaurant. Due to the closeness in their ages Jennie had been too young when he was a baby to remember exactly what he had been like and so hadn't made the connection her mum just did.

'I try to tell people what Marcel's like mum, but nobody believes me. They seem to think I am exaggerating or just not coping.' Jennie's exasperation was apparent in the tone of her voice.

'Well if he is another Tommy, there isn't a blind thing you

84

can do about it sweetie so you'd best just carry on as you are. He could still grow out of it, maybe he is anxious from being born so early? I am so proud of you; I never imagined you would make such a good Mummy!' Tears welled in her eyes as Jennie flung herself into her mother's arms.

Jennie had always been a difficult, headstrong child but becoming a mother seemed to have made a world of difference in her attitude. Sabi's lips curved up in a delighted grin. She could count on the fingers of both hands the amount of times Jennie had listened to her advice and accepted it, without fierce debate. Few enough times to mean this one was a novelty to be pondered many times and enjoyed. Luckily there was a National Tarmac Championship on, which meant she would be spared the company of the man Jennie had chosen to marry for most of her visit. Sabi did worry that Stephen's continued absences were putting Jennie under unmanageable strain. Sabi worried that Jennie was heading for an emotional fall out. She watched her daughter run herself ragged caring for Marcel, refusing most offers of help, explaining that she'd got into a routine and didn't want to get used to having help or she might not be able to cope on her own again when Sabi left. Sabi was loathe to interfere, scared it would alienate Jennie from her but couldn't help worrying that she was failing in her own duty as Jennie's mother. Her stomach would clench with despair as she watched Jennie rush down the stairs to fetch Marcel, feed him, change him and do whatever else was needed to settle him on a seemingly continuous loop. To Sabi, she seemed to be on the knife-edge of depression, somehow managing to keep her balance without falling off and into the abyss. Stephen was away working on the rally working late into the evening on weekdays, some nights he didn't come home at all and on the weekends he made the excuse of going round to Simon and Sue's for the evening so that she and Jennie could have "mother and daughter time". Sabi wasn't fooled by Stephen blaming too much alcohol or a movie ending really late as the reasons for not coming home to sleep at night. If Jennie wasn't so worn out all the time she might be able to recognise the danger signs too.

The question was, how did she break the news to Jennie that she was sure Stephen was having an affair? Given half a chance she'd snatch both Jennie and Marcel up and take them back home with her. The sun was already warm in the Okanagan this time of the year and so much healthier for one's spirit than this land of cloud that England existed as in early May. That waste of skin Jennie called a husband probably wouldn't even miss them, she thought angrily. She hadn't seen him so much as lift a finger, whenever he was actually home, in the week and a half that she'd been there. How Jennie coped (the house was always pointlessly spotless) she couldn't imagine and she had a good mind to speak sternly to him before she left next week.

It was no secret that Stephen and Sabi disliked each other. He was so obviously not Jennie's usual type that her mother had queried the attraction from the start. Jennie never could explain it to her mother's or her own satisfaction. In hindsight, Jennie knew it had been her biological time clock ticking and she guessed her mother assumed the same. Of course they hadn't discussed this, Jennie wasn't a great one for meaningful conversations. That much hadn't changed though perhaps it would, given enough time, Sabi thought hopefully.

Jennie's heart melted as she watched her mother smooth her cheek against the top of Marcel's head as she snuggled him against her shoulder. Her mother clearly adored Marcel and he seemed so much calmer when he was near his grandmother. Marcel would go limp with contentment when listening to her make that odd resonant noise deep in her throat. Jennie delighted in being able to witness this side of Marcel though she felt a bit of a failure for not being able to cause the same reaction in him more frequently. However, the joy on her mother's face as she gazed at Marcel was a sight she would never tire of.

Nineteen

Her Mum's holiday was almost over and the thought of her leaving them made Jennie feel bereaved. How would she cope without her mum's advice? She hadn't realized how much she needed her until then. The day before they'd taken Marcel out for a car ride in an attempt to soothe his angry crying. Jennie's mum was trying to show her ways to distract Marcel into calming down, without giving in to his demands for constant cuddles. They drove around for an hour with Marcel raging in the backseat until neither of them could take anymore and they pulled over on the seafront to cuddle and soothe Marcel's nerves and their own. The thudding of the waves breaking on the shore was a nice counterpoint to their sense of agitation and gradually their frantic heartbeats slowed and their ears stopped ringing. Jennie fed Marcel and watched the roiling water as white caps were whipped up on the tops of the waves by the wind.

'How can two grown women be so controlled by an infant?' said her mother in a puzzled tone. 'I was always just as firm with you and you responded so well to it. In fact you were a delight as a baby, sleeping through the night from 5 weeks old!'

'Oh Mum, don't!' groaned Jennie, envious at the mere thought of a full night's sleep.

'Well Jennie I can't think of any other tips for you. Can't you ask the health visitors for some advice? Didn't I hear the last one mention a sleep clinic or something?'

Jennie thought back fuzzily through the haze of tiredness and the heaviness of the atmosphere that always seemed to descend as Marcel succumbed reluctantly to sleep.

'Do you mean the one who did Marcel's last health check? Yes I think she did say something about a sleep clinic but that was for babies who are much older, mum. I think that was for ones who are already old enough to be in their own rooms!' Jennie and her mum lapsed into silence, lulled by the sound of the waves resounding through the open windows.

Jennie sensed her mum scrutinising her. She tipped her head sideways on the seat and made eye contact with the full wattage of her mum's luminous green eyes.

'Mum! Why are you staring?' Jennie winced as she heard the juvenile whinging undertone to her voice.

Her mum wisely resisted the urge to snap out a remark she'd instantly regret and instead closed her eyes while still facing Jennie.

'Sorry,' Jennie mumbled, feeling the tears begin to well and desperately wanting to lie across the seat and rest her head on her mum's lap. She could almost sense the sound her mother's fingers would make as the brushed past her ears while smoothing her hair.

'Jennie… this is the last time I will bring this up but please promise me you will consider asking Stephen to go for some marriage counselling. It's no secret that I dislike the man but if you truly love him and want to make a go of this then you need to sort the problems out before they grow.'

'Mum! We've been through a lot in such a short time; I don't think it's fair of you to expect us to behave like other newlyweds,' Jennie exclaimed, instantly on the defensive.

Undeterred, her mum continued, 'I do think it is strange you two are having problems so early on in your relationship but as you said, perhaps it is all a case of "too much too soon" for you both. Finally, I have to say that I am sure I am not so objectionable that I can cause a new husband and father to prefer to sleep at his friends whenever he is home from work instead of beside his new wife.'

Jennie nodded with her eyes squeezed shut to prevent the tears escaping when her mother stopped speaking. She was afraid that if she started crying, she would not be able to stop. Where had her blissful bubble gone? She had an unhappy baby, an absent husband and her mother's holiday with them was almost at an end. How would she cope without her mum's warmth, support and sensible, if not always appreciated, advice? Her mum had mentioned more than once during her pregnancy that she could bring "the baby" and live with her. Although comforting, the concept made her cringe, she was a grown woman and could not imagine that living with her mother would be any more pleasant than it had been as a teenager. Jennie knew that running away with her mum wasn't an option. *I've made my bed with Stephen and I'm just going to have to continue lying in it. It's time to act like an adult instead of shirking my responsibilities*, she told herself firmly.

Twenty

Stephen smiled his thanks at Sue for the good nosh, leaned back in his chair and winked at Simon. Pushing aside the waves of sadness that kept trying to overcome him, Stephen reflected on the fact that his pal had landed on his feet without a doubt. Stephen wished that Jennie could be more like Sue. Sue always seemed up for a laugh and kept the house neat as a pin and herself well made up. Stephen knew deep down that even if Jennie was more like Sue, it wouldn't be enough to fix all that was wrong with their marriage. All that he knew he had made wrong with their marriage. The glue holding together his relationship, such as it was, with Jennie was his love for Marcel and nothing more.

'How is Jennie getting on? Seems like ages since we've seen her! I don't like to phone in case I interrupt her at a crucial moment with Marcel.' *And his constant crying makes my nerves jangle*, she thought to herself. Sue did miss her friend; nights out with Simon and Stephen were great but couldn't replace the pleasure of sharing a bottle or two of wine and some girlie talk with Jennie. *It's a shame Jennie lost the ability to do girl talk as soon as she fell pregnant, ever since then all she's done is talk about baby things, it's no wonder I don't feel comfortable making conversation with her anymore*, Sue groused to herself.

'Ah she isn't the same Jennie you introduced me to,' Stephen said mournfully, unaware that Jennie thought exactly the same about him.

'Well we thought there must be something wrong when you came to party on Valentine's Day without Jennie, is the kiddie getting to you?' laughed Simon.

'Nah my little man is just the best, though Jennie seems to think there is something wrong with him because he plays her up sometimes by not settling. He can cry for hours if he's in a mood that boy of mine. I keep reminding her that the midwife said that all little 'uns have unsettled times but she's not satisfied,' Stephen puffed out his cheeks and then exhaled with pent up frustration.

'Her mum doesn't go back for a couple more days and there is no talking any sense into Jennie while her mum is meddling and encouraging her.' Stephen's face fell into a sneer of dislike which mirrored his feelings for Jennie's mum.

'Mate, if you're finding it that hard with her why don't you just kick her out?' Simon was puzzled by his pal's apparent desire to further complicate his life.

'Cos she's the mother of my son and I'm not risking losing contact with him. I've waited a long time for him and I intend to do my best to make sure I am an on hand dad.' With that Stephen crossed his arms, tucked his chin into his chest and made a silly face which got the other two laughing and him out of the spotlight.

Stephen is such a gem, with that great sense of humour, thought Sue. She'd have to have a quiet word with Jennie and let her know what she was risking by not taking better care of Stephen. It was unlike Jennie to be so careless and unkind.

Grasping at the thought which tried to flutter past the recesses of her memory, Sue said, 'Not that I am making excuses for her, Stephen, but maybe Jennie is having a hard time coping with the added complication in your life? It's taken me a while to get used to the whole concept and I don't have any kids to complicate things! Jennie never mentions it to me and she is such an open minded, generous person that I just assumed she was okay about it.' *And,* thought Sue, *I don't want to be the one who has to tell Jennie about Stephen's spent driving conviction when we struggle to find any mutually interesting and pleasant subjects to talk about as it is since Jennie became a mum!*

Stephen and Simon quickly flicked sideways glances at her and then each other.

Baffled by their behaviour, Sue said, 'Why are you looking at each other like that? Stephen? You have told Jennie about Alice?'

The sound of the fridge humming became very loud in the ensuing silence, which rushed to fill the vacuum left by the men as they exited the room.

'Oh shit!' Sue mumbled as the full impact of this complication hit her. While she did understand Stephen's reasons for wanting to be a part of Alice's life she had assumed he would tell Jennie about her. If she was honest it had been easier to think Stephen would tell her than to do it herself but a true friend wouldn't have taken the easy way out. Sue knew she had crossed another invisible line and betrayed her friend by proxy for the second time. First by withholding her knowledge about Stephen's conviction and now this. Sue also knew that if Jennie found out the part she had inadvertently played in this deceit she would never forgive her. What Sue didn't know was the extent to which Alice had become a part of Stephen's life. Stephen hadn't told Simon or Sue that he had grown to feel that Alice made him whole.

Part Two

Twenty one

Alice paused before going through her gate. The scent of the orange blossom shrub deserved a moment's quiet appreciation and she was reluctant to move on until she heard the reassuring sound of the front door of her two bedroom bungalow closing. That hydraulic hinge was a marvel and saved her going to the effort of pulling the door shut behind her but it took her a long time to get used to novelties, no matter how clever they might be. She left her gate open and turned right along the pavement. Her cupboards were looking sorry for themselves and the fridge seemed to mock her with the gleam off its bare shelves. Food shopping was always a chore that she avoided until the last possible moment but she'd be eating flour paste if she waited another day so she knew she had to get it over with today or suffer the expense of another pizza delivery.

'Hello Alice! How's you this fine day?'

'Mr Desderman, how lovely to see you!' Alice smiled.

He had been friends with her parents for as long as she could remember. It was rare for her to pass his house without seeing him loitering in his courtyard. Always dressed as if he were on his way to work, in a suit and tie with his hair slicked back from his brow; he greeted all the residents of their street in the same fond tone of voice. His ancient black Labrador bestowed soft woofs and licks on anyone who got within range of his tongue. Like his master, old Bert loved all who brightened their day by choosing to stop and spend a few moments with them. Bert had a particular fondness for people like Alice who took the time to scratch behind his soft ears.

'I haven't seen that man of yours around recently, away with work again is he?' A wistful note crept into Mr Desderman's voice for he had retired early and now found he missed the reassuring routine of work. He longed to relive the time when he had begun each day with a sense of purpose instead of this endless waiting and wondering whether it would be himself or his lovely old Bert who would be the first to pass on to the golden land.

'I expect he'll be home in a day or two...' Alice paused on seeing the sadness pass over her neighbour's eyes and settle onto his face. Assuming he was missing the company of his wife, dead more than three years now, Alice continued, 'I find evenings so lonely without him Mr Desderman, would you be so kind as to join me for supper this evening? We could eat in the garden so Bert could come as well without disturbing the cats overly much.'

'A splendid idea young lady! What time would you like us?' His eyes brightened at this unexpected invitation.

'Shall we say 6pm? It will still be warm in the garden then. I'll probably be out there before that time so why don't you take my spare key so you can let yourself in? That way I won't have to worry about not hearing you knock.'

Alice fiddled with the key for a few seconds until she gave up in frustration and passed the ring to Mr Desderman. 'My fingernails are such a hindrance with things like this!'

He swiftly removed the key and handed the rest back to her with a generous smile, 'Your fingernails are the perfect complement to such beautiful hands.'

'Well I'd best be getting the shopping done so I can have our meal ready in time.' Alice felt much more inclined to do this task now that she had someone besides herself to attend to.

A look of concern passed over Mr Desderman's face, 'Would you like me to come and give you a hand with the shopping? Will you manage to get it all home on your own?'

'Not to worry, if I buy too much then I will call for a taxi as usual!' With one lingering stroke of Bert's head and a cheery wave to Mr Desderman, Alice made her way to the mayhem of the nearest superstore.

Mr Desderman stood beside Bert and watched her till she turned the corner. Young Alice was such a wonderful person, never anything but outwardly cheerful despite all the challenges and sorrow that had been thrown her way in the past several years. His admiration of her surpassed description.

Twenty two

Alice grimaced at the greasy feel under the dishcloth as she washed the last of the BBQ tools they had used last night. They had sat wrapped in blankets watching the evening sky until Alice was lulled into a most pleasant stupor. Washing up had been the furthest thing on her mind as she said goodnight to Mr Desderman and she had made her way directly to bed after closing the front door. Alice smiled as she finished the last of her chores. Chores they might be but the satisfaction of completing them was worth all the effort. Her wood floors gleamed and a few lingering dust motes danced in the brightly lit front room, resisting the draught from the open windows. Her soul felt as if it too was dancing; flitting around the room in joyful abandon in time with the flashes of sun that snuck in through the curtains flutters and flashed in golden sparkles along the still damp floor. She'd had a text from her darling man and he would be home that night. She had never expected to find love with someone so dissimilar but she now knew the truth in the saying, "opposites attract". Boy did they ever and to think that they met in such unusual circumstances. The clatter of her letter slot distracted Alice from her musings and she shouted 'Just a minute!' as she began to make her way towards the door.

Peering through the spy hole, she smiled as she saw the yellow flower on the other side. Opening the door, she took the rose and thanked the delivery person for the fifth time that week. For years now her darling had sent her a yellow rose from the neighbourhood florist each day, the message on this one said, "Missing you big time" and was surrounded by kisses. Soppy maybe but it worked for her. He always sent her yellow roses because they signified friendship and joy. He said they had been friends long before they were lovers and that her friendship had always made him joyful. After all she'd been through in the past few years, sentiments like that felt like a healing balm, gave her something to live for.

The day passed and the shadows began to lengthen the ends of the room. Alice's heart leapt as she heard his key in the door.

'Alice? Where are you flower? I need a kiss and a hug, woman!'

'In the kitchen darling! Alice lifted her face to meet Stephen's kiss as he leant over her wheelchair and wrapped his arms around her upper back.

They laughed as one of the cats tried to squeeze between their arms for a share of the affection. They too missed Stephen when he was away for he always made a fuss of them and would spend hours tantalizing them with their toys or smoothing their fur while they purred contentedly. Werecat (so named because she would run around meowling during a full moon) would follow him around when he was home, contentedly looking at him and saying 'meep', as if she had used up her quota of meows during her last full moon rampage. Mojo would sulk until Stephen had grovelled to a level he deemed sufficient and then would not leave his side until it was time for Stephen to insult him by vacating the house again.

The only blight on her happiness nowadays was her desire to have a child, to make the circle of their love complete. However, the trying to get pregnant part was very enjoyable indeed and Alice could tell from the glint in Stephen's eyes that there was a lot of pleasure in store for her tonight.

Alice grinned and said, 'Is it bed time yet?'

'Bed? We don't need a bed! We are going to be a little creative with seating arrangements on that saddle seat, I've always wondered why you bought it but I think I know a way to put it to good use... and the sooner the better!' Stephen murmured in her ear. His words alone sent flickering tendrils of lust through her, supper could wait till they'd taken the edge off their appetite for each other.

Twenty three

To say the day that she and Stephen had met was a momentous one would be an understatement. She was still able to walk with ease back then but, like most people, she did not appreciate that blessing until it was taken away. Without a car and wanting to shop in the neighbouring city, she'd called a taxi rather than take the train and then walk the half mile to the shopping precinct. Alice had always been sociable and found herself enjoying an easy banter with the cabbie, laughing often at his humorous perspective on life's twists and challenges. She was vaguely aware of the speed the cab was going at and felt momentary regret that the trip would be over sooner than she would like. Wondering if she could arrange for him to be driving the cab which took her home, she enquired as to when his shift finished that day. Neither of them noticed the van drifting across into their lane until the moment of impact.

Alice regained complete consciousness several days later. Prior to that she had drifted in and out of floaty morphine fuelled dreams, unaware of much besides the pain that grew and faded but never diminished entirely and that her parents were at her beside. It was several more before she realised the extent of the damage done to her hips and internal organs.

'You have a fractured skull and we kept you heavily sedated until the swelling went down. Your pelvis was broken in three places. We've managed to pin it together but may need to adjust them as you heal. Unfortunately there was some nerve damage done and you'll need some help from the physiotherapists before you will be able to walk properly again.'

Numb until she heard this sentence Alice said, 'But I will walk okay eventually?'

'If you put the effort into it anything is possible, we start the process off by putting the pieces of the puzzle back together but you've got to be the one to put in the hard physical work.'

Alice asked after the driver of the cab who she had retained a mind's picture of with his head thrown back laughing at something she had said.

'You needn't worry about him, he's had what was coming to him, the police arrested him in A&E for driving while under the influence of alcohol and for causing grievous bodily harm to you.' The doctor smiled as if he had been personally responsible for this arrest.

'He was drunk? Impossible!' Alice's eyes opened wide in shock; surely she would have known if he was drunk?

'His blood alcohol levels told the truth and he's been given a nine month sentence.' The doctor looked smug.

'The accident wasn't even his fault though, I remember a white van coming into our lane!'

'Witnesses say the van driver was signalling before he changed lanes and that your taxi stayed put. The police have enough evidence from eye witnesses and the motorway cameras to believe that the taxi driver was at fault.'

What a load of rubbish! Alice thought angrily. She'd been in the car not the police. She resolved to contact the taxi driver once she was discharged and assure him she did not blame him for the accident.

'Do you know what the driver's name was by any chance?'

'Yep, Stephen Copeland. If you want to send him hate mail I am sure Victim's Support will give you some way of getting a letter to him. People like him often don't realize the extent of the damage they cause by their selfishness unless they hear from the people whose lives they have ruined.'

'S'cuse me for asking but has this happened to you?' Alice was sure there had to be a reason he sounded so personally involved in her injuries and delighted at Mr Copeland's conviction.

'Yes, my son. He wasn't as lucky as you though, he died of his injuries.'

'I am sorry.'

'Yes, so am I. So… anyway, enough about my tragedy, back to you, try to make the most of this precious life you've been given.' He patted Alice's shoulder and walked away.

Twenty four

A few years before Alice's accident, her parents had gone to Nepal on what they had intended to be a one year experience as English teachers. After the initial culture shock passed, they both grew to love the country and were now settled permanently in Kathmandu which was in the heavily urbanised southern region of Nepal. Demand for English classes within the multilingual society kept them securely employed though poorly paid by English standards.

Mid morning on the day Alice was injured Fern had settled herself onto the wooden bench outside the school and placed her mint tea beside her before taking out her mobile to send Gary a text. He was working that evening and it was his turn to sort supper for them. He was turning into an excellent cook and Fern couldn't resist asking him what delights he had in store for her. She turned her mobile on, thanking whatever powers it was that had created the mobile because landlines in Nepal were rare and unreliable at best but mobiles worked well in most parts of the country. Fern's heart sank when she noticed that she had a missed call from Art Desderman. If Art had made the effort to phone then it had to be important and more than likely would be bad news. He hated using phones and although they got emails on a regular basis from their old friend, the last phone call they had from him had been when his wife died. Just as she was about to phone Art back, Gary called her explaining that Art had phoned Fern first assuming that Gary would be working, then realised his mistake when he was prompted to leave a message. Instead he'd phoned Gary to break the news that Alice was in hospital and although still unconscious, her health was considered stable. The worst damage she had suffered was to her head and to her pelvis, both of which were fractured in a road traffic accident. Fern listened as Gary spoke, feeling hollow and frantic. She was desperate to end the conversation so she could take the necessary steps towards getting back to England.

'Fern? Honey, please say something so I know you are ok,'

Gary pleaded, worried that Fern might have fainted.

'I'm here Gary, obviously I'm *not* ok because I'm here and I *want* to be in England!' Gary could hear the slightly hysterical note to her voice beginning to peak before Fern paused and took a deep breath.

'I know darling. We'll be with Alice as fast as possible, we'll leave today if we can.'

'Gary?' Fern's voice faltered then came back stronger, 'Remember when the midwife came to tell us that Alice probably had Down's syndrome and we had to go for that horrible test?'

'Yes, I do, all too well.'

'Well she was fine then and I *know* she's going to be fine now, our girl's a fighter.' Hope flared in Fern's chest as she spoke those words. That horrible experience had turned out well and she refused to accept that this outcome could be any different.

'That she is.' Gary's voice sounded odd even to him. A mixture of hope, fear and anger he decided.

'I'll let the school know and then I'll be home.' Fern promised.

'I'll phone the airport and start packing. Love you.'

'Love you too, bye for now.'

Fern and Gary took comfort from the tasks they'd delegated themselves over the phone. Those first steps towards bringing order and predictability back into their lives. Using as few words as possible in an attempt to make it less real, Fern informed the school principal that they would be taking an indefinite leave of absence and why. Then she got on her bike and rode home to hug her husband before they finished packing all that they'd need for their trip back to England. Flights from Nepal left on a regular basis but connections to flights going to England were more difficult to coordinate and they endured two arduous days of travelling before they arrived in England.

Twenty five

Fern and Gary arrived at the hospital exhausted. Art had taken their bags from them and gone to store them in his car so that they could have some time alone with Alice. Art had found out Alice was in hospital when he'd popped round mid morning the day after the accident, expecting to have a cup of tea with Alice on her day off as arranged, only to hear the cats frantic at the door and a stack of post visible on the floor through the letterbox. He used the key Alice had given him for emergencies, fed the cats and gathered up the post. After a look round the house to make sure Alice wasn't lying in one of the rooms, injured in some way, he'd phoned the hospital to ask if Alice had been admitted. They refused to give him any information besides saying that there was someone named Alice Redwood currently registered as an inpatient. He'd managed to convince them to allow him to be with Alice until her parents arrived by telling them he was her uncle and explaining that her parents were in Nepal. What he neglected to tell the hospital staff was that there was no genetic blood tie between himself and the Redwoods. Art volunteered to be the one who told Fern and Gary the news.

He'd warned Fern and Gary that Alice was fading in and out of consciousness but that the doctors had said this was due to the morphine she was being given for pain rather than anything more sinister as Fern and Gary had feared. The attending consultant had left word that he would visit first thing the next morning to explain things in further detail but they thought Art had already done a pretty good job of detailing Alice's injuries when they'd phoned him for an update during their first stop over on the trip to England. Three hairline fractures of the pelvis, broken ribs, concussion and a single skull fracture, extensive bruising, and internal damage to an ovary. They'd listened horrified that she was so damaged, intensely grateful that the doctors were confident she'd heal. For the next week one of them was always at Alice's bedside, both Fern and Gary during the day but at night one of them would dose fitfully on a chair beside Alice's bed, holding her hand all night while the other went back to Alice's to sleep at night and to make a fuss of the cats. Art came and kept them company each day at the hospital and also did his share of keeping the cats amused. The week after they arrived Alice was awake and fully conscious as her pain medication dose had been lowered. Fern and Gary, on the consultant's advice began to both go back to Alice's to sleep at night. Alice was beginning to shift herself around in bed now and had been told that the next day she would be encouraged to get up and out of her bed. They could see she was on the mend but what none of them knew was how gruelling the recovery process would be.

The next day Fern and Gary arrived at the hospital feeling anxious and concerned over the fact that Alice was expected to get out of bed today when just shifting around in bed caused her pain. Alice was sitting up in bed and burst into tears as soon as they walked through the door.

'I can't do it, I hurt already,' she sobbed.

'Oh darling,' Fern walked to the bed, dropped her bag on the floor and smoothed Alice's hair. Gary followed her, pushed her bag under the bed with his foot and reached around Fern to hand Alice a wad of tissues.

'Thanks dad. Please tell them I can't do it, that I'm not ready.' Alice composed herself by wiping firmly at her eyes.

'Honey, if the doctors think you're ready then you have to trust them. You can't stay in bed forever.' Gary walked round to the other side of the bed, pulling the bed curtains with him to hide Alice from the view of the rest of the room's occupants. He patted Alice's shoulder and looked across at Fern for help.

'Besides, Alice, you want to get rid of that don't you?' Fern indicated the tube which snaked out from under the blankets to the bag of urine suspended from a stand which rested on the floor.

'Yes but I'm scared that'll hurt too. Everything hurts enough already.' Alice bust into tears again.

'Hello?' called a voice from behind the curtains swiftly

followed by a smiling face haloed with curls.

'Hi?' Alice said. Fern and Gary nodded but said nothing.

'I'm Sandy. I'm a physiotherapist and I'm going to be spending some time with you each day this week to get you up and walking round on these.' Sandy lifted a pair of crutches and smiled again.

'Today?' Alice spluttered. 'But, I've not even got out of bed yet!'

'Yes today, later on this afternoon you're going to have a go at standing up on your own holding onto the back of your bedside chair. This morning the nurses will help you out of bed and sitting on your chair and I'll be back later after you've had a chance to get used to that.'

Sandy left and soon after two nurses arrived. Fern and Gary went for coffee while the nurses removed Alice's catheter and got her sat up in her bedside chair. When they came back fifteen minutes later Alice was in bed.

'What's happened?' Fern asked anxiously.

'We expected to see you sat up in your chair!' Gary clarified.

'I was but I kept fainting so they've put me back in bed for a while,' Alice saw the looks of horror on her parent's faces and said hastily 'The nurses told me it's normal to feel faint at first.' She yawned hugely. 'That really wore me out! They said I could try again after lunch. I'm quite looking forward to it, fainting or no fainting, it was nice to be upright for a bit and even though it did hurt it wasn't anywhere near as painful as I'd feared.'

From that afternoon on Alice moved from strength to strength, growing in confidence about her abilities to move about until she could manage to do so unassisted for short periods of time. By the time Alice was discharged from hospital twelve days later, Gary had been told that he had to return to Nepal as the school would only agree to one of them taking an extended leave of absence. Fern stayed to care for Alice as she continued the long slow process of recovery. Alice struggled to walk any distance due to the pain which would flare up if she moved about too much and

Alice found that she had to use a wheelchair more often than not. The doctors seemed puzzled but hastily assured her that this shouldn't be a permanent problem. Physiotherapists worked with her to strengthen her body while the occupational therapists helped Alice to train herself to get in and out of her wheelchair. The damage to her hips was considerable enough that she found she couldn't walk any distance and she began to rely more and more on her wheelchair. Much to her disgust the physiotherapist said this was likely down to the fear of the pain than a true necessity and that in time she would not need her chair at all. Her mother and the doctor had said similar she remembered, but it was easy for them to say, they didn't have to endure the unendurable misery that her body had become. Each physio session left her feeling as if she was swathed in layers of pain and even without the physical insult of physiotherapy she still hurt at the end of each day. Simple everyday tasks vexed her beyond belief. One of the pins in her hip tweaked a nerve whenever she sat for extended periods of time, which was annoying enough to keep her moving on a regular basis. It served a purpose in that respect, Fern told Alice, only to be rewarded with a baleful look. Although Alice enjoyed the hydrotherapy in the physio department, she longed for the day when she would be able to get into and out of her bath without help. This desperation gave her the will power to attend the more painful land based physio sessions and to put herself through additional mobility exercises at home.

In the months after her discharge, Alice had to endure more surgery, this time to remove one of her ovaries which had been badly damaged in the accident. Although the surgeons had tried to repair it during her first bout of surgery, it persisted in bleeding on occasion which caused Alice considerable unnecessary pain. The surgeons agreed, reassured her that she still had a possibility of falling pregnant with one ovary, that the offending one would be of no use in that respect and removed it.

Twenty six

After Alice had recovered from her surgery she contacted Victim Support to try and trace Stephen Copeland. They informed her that he had been convicted of dangerous driving causing grievous bodily harm and was serving a prison sentence. Following the compulsion that she had felt so strongly in the days after the accident, she composed a careful letter explaining that she bore him no ill will and thought it outrageous that he had been convicted. Although Alice had broached this subject with her mother, Fern was inclined to disagree. The rage that Fern had felt towards Stephen Copeland in the first few weeks after the accident had faded slightly as Alice began to recover but it would flare up on occasion as she watched her daughter struggle with tasks which she had once performed effortlessly. Fern felt that the man who had, allegedly unintentionally, put her daughter in hospital deserved to be convicted and that as long as he was in jail he couldn't harm anyone else. Alice knew of her mother's feelings about this and after heatedly debating the issue at length they agreed to disagree. Alice was an adult and Fern decided to respect her right to do as she pleased in relation to Mr Copeland though Fern reserved the right to not be happy about it. On one of Alice's more painful days, Fern composed a letter of her own to Mr Copeland telling him that she thought he was a menace who deserved to be locked up and without telling Alice, copied the address off Alice's letter when she went to post it for her.

Two letters dropped through the letterbox a week later while Alice was enjoying a hydrotherapy session. Fern picked up the post on her way through the door before stepping aside into the front room in order to allow Alice enough room to manoeuvre the wheelchair into the house. Alice was using the chair less frequently now but always relied on it after physio sessions which seemed to leave her exhausted and in pain. Tucking the letter addressed to her into her handbag, Fern turned around to hand Alice the rest of the post.

'Cup of tea?'

'Yes please mum.'

Fern made her way to the kitchen leaving Alice to get settled on the couch. While the kettle boiled she read her letter from Mr Copeland. It was short and neatly written and contained an apology for the grief he had caused them all and for the pain he had unintentionally caused Alice through his own stupidity. He made no excuses, which Fern appreciated. He also assured her that he knew now to never drink more than a pint if he knew he would be driving the morning after and he invited her to write again if she felt that she had anything else to say. Fern thought back to all the times she and Gary had been out for meals and enjoyed several glasses of wine, never giving a second thought to the fact that they might not be safe to drive the following morning. She didn't know that Stephen had been spiralling into a serious drink problem before the accident. With a sinking heart, Fern realised that this accident was one which could reasonably happen to anyone. She didn't want to and couldn't forgive this man who had damaged her daughter even though she thought that she probably should. However, being logical and actually managing not to hate this man who had hurt her Alice were different things entirely. Fern decided that a letter of apology was an easy thing to write, he certainly had ample time to sit and think how to phrase his letter to her. She wasn't convinced that he had learnt the error of his ways so fast. Time and his behaviour once released from prison will tell the true story, Fern decided. Perhaps in time she could forgive him but Fern knew she would never forget. Fern made a mental note to share her slight change in perspective with Alice that evening. She finished making the tea and brought a cup into Alice.

'Here you go darling, I'm taking mine upstairs because I want to email your dad.'

''K mum, ta.' Alice smile up at her and returned her attention to the letter she was reading. Fern guessed it was from Mr Copeland because she recognised the handwriting.

Alice was delighted to find that Stephen was as humorous

via the written word as he had been in real life. The first line of his response to her initial letter had said *'Dear Alice, I was pleasantly surprised to get a letter from you though I have to admit I was a bit worried it would burst into angry flames when I opened it!'* She giggled at the image this created.

Fern had taken to Skyping Gary because it allowed her to talk to him as often as she needed to without the expense of a mobile phone call. Today she chose to email him so that she could get her thoughts out in as orderly a fashion as possible. In about twenty minutes she'd typed in a précis of the contents of Mr Copeland's letter and her reaction to it. The four hour time difference meant it was early evening in Kathmandu and Gary responded within minutes to say that although he agreed that Mr Copeland was probably not the hardened criminal they had pictured, he wasn't sure he could come to terms with the fact that the man who injured Alice might actually be a nice person and that he needed to hate someone for hurting their girl. He asked Fern to scan the letter and email it to him. Fern did so and then sat back admiring the advances in technology that facilitated her communication with her husband at this level of intricacy when he was over four and a half thousand miles away.

Fern sighed. *Intricate communication is fabulous in its own right*, she thought, *but it isn't the intimate conversation that I want with Gary and I am starting to miss more and more.* She went down to speak to Alice, marvelling at the inner strength and clarity of perception that she had shown. Alice had instinctively given Mr Copeland more credit as a human being than either her or Gary had and it was a lesson learned that Fern intended to take to heart and, one which she intended to thank her daughter for.

108

Twenty seven

Soon Alice and Stephen were writing twice weekly and chatting on the phone once a month, though he didn't get long on the prison phone because there was always a queue of men waiting to use it after him. Fern and Alice had long conversations about Alice's feelings for Stephen. Fern worried that Alice was becoming too attached and that she needed to let go in order to move on from that damaging experience, but Alice explained that she felt there was an odd but pleasant symbiosis to healing while in contact with the man who had been with her when she was injured. Fern knew that Alice was convinced this was the way forward for her and she saw Alice visibly brighten whenever she got a letter from Stephen. Alice told Fern that she felt that having a pen pal helped make her recovery more worthwhile, gave her a reason to strive towards meeting the increasing demands set for her during the gruelling physio appointments. There were no awkward, boredom filled, pauses in written conversations and she poured out her struggles without worrying that she was becoming repetitive. *After all*, Alice thought, *if he didn't like it, he didn't have to read it and I'd be none the wiser.* Fern wondered why Alice didn't feel that speaking to her provided the same impetus to heal but didn't ask knowing instinctively that Alice wanted something different than the support which her mother was already giving her. Alice rejoiced for Stephen when he was released early for good behaviour and they continued to write to each other with the phone calls increasing in frequency to once a week.

Stephen and Alice began to meet once a month for lunch or an afternoon outing. Fern fretted from the sidelines, worrying that Alice was getting deeper into a relationship that might be unhealthy. She knew her daughter had a kind soul and an innate ability to sense the hidden good in people but Fern worried that this time Alice had gotten it wrong. Fern Skyped Gary when Alice was out with Stephen one afternoon to discuss her growing concerns. She wondered if

Alice needed counselling but was afraid to voice it to her without sounding Gary out about it first.

'I could just about cope with the written contact between them because I know what Alice is like, she needs to be kind to others, it's just how she's made.'

'I'm happy to admit that I'm not at all comfortable about them meeting in person though,' Gary sighed.

'I'm glad it's not just me being an overprotective mum.'

'But that's just it, maybe it is because we are over-protective parents now. We haven't had an urge to 'vet' the men she spends time with for years.'

'Well we've been in another country so it would have been difficult!' They both laughed.

'No, in all seriousness though Fern, maybe we'd feel different if we met Stephen, maybe he really is a nice guy?'

'Yeah... a really nice guy who got shitfaced drunk and thought he'd head off to work before the alcohol had worn off so that he could damage our girl!' Fern said bitterly.

'Yup, that's the problem for us. I can't imagine we'll ever be able to move past that and I've no idea how Alice has managed to,' Gary continued. 'She's an adult, Fern, we've got to keep reminding ourselves of that. Maybe we're struggling because we are having to have blind faith in Alice's judgement of Stephen's character and all we've got to go on is his actions on the day he hurt her.'

'But, she's getting into a relationship with someone who hurt her badly. Someone who was sent to jail for it! What if she's got Stockholm syndrome?' said Fern referring to the cognitive dissonance that allows some victims to begin to identify with and become loyal to those who have hurt them.

'I think Stockholm syndrome is linked to victims who were held hostage for long periods of time. Alice went through a different experience altogether. You know I've talked to her at length about this. I've told her that I don't understand her motives in relation to Stephen nor do I like the fact that she is spending more time with him. But from what I can tell from speaking with her and from everything else you've told me over the past few months she sounds as if she is

110

emotionally 'all right', pretty much like the Alice she was before the accident.'

Despite her parents' discomfort with the concept of her growing friendship with Stephen, Alice continued to nurture their relationship. Following her physiotherapist's and mother's advice, Alice refused to accept Stephen's offer of a lift to the restaurants, park, cinema, or wherever they had decided to meet on that day. Instead she chose to make her own way there as part of her ongoing recovery. Doing so gave her confidence on both emotional and physical levels. It did not, however, lessen her pain and neither did the physio sessions to any large extent.

Twenty eight

The physical anguish that Alice still experienced on a daily basis was extreme in her opinion. *Surely I should have improved beyond this level of aching, burning muscular angst?* she wondered. It affected both sides of her body, okay if pushed, she was happy to admit it wasn't on every inch of her body, but it did involve much of her arms, legs, and everywhere in between, including these damn headaches which made her feel as if someone was hitting her between the eyes with a ball peen hammer. Alice made repeated visits to her GP to complain, to beg for stronger painkillers, none of which helped to any extent. Living in constant pain was getting her down and Alice began to doubt herself. She worried that she was becoming a hypochondriac and that her pain was all in her mind, and she was beginning to suspect her GP thought so too.

Eventually on one of her visits to the physiotherapist she said in desperation, 'My whole body feels like a sprained ankle! Exercise hurts but it does give me a tiny bit of relief afterwards. The problem is that the longer I rest, the more it hurts, and getting out of bed in the morning is akin to torture because I get so stiff overnight. Surely I am entitled to rest during the night? Heat makes the pain worse; if I get cold I am in agony, I even ache under my fingernails!' Alice's voice rose higher with each sentence and to her dismay she felt tears prickling her eyes.

'Excuse me?' asked a voice from behind the curtain that her physio had pulled round the examination area in order to give Alice a bit of privacy while she had her muscles poked, prodded and manipulated.

'Hello?' said her physio and another therapist peered round the curtain with a smile for Alice.

'I was walking past and overheard you describing your symptoms… I am no expert in medical diagnosis of course but I do have a patient with a condition called Fibromyalgia who complains of almost identical aches and pains. Have you ever heard of Fibromyalgia?'

Alice shook her head.

'I'll see if I can find one of the leaflets on the condition, be back shortly.'

Within a few minutes the physio was back, 'Here, have a read of this and if you think it applies to you then best let your GP know so that you can be referred to a specialist for assessment!'

Desperately hoping to find a reason for her pain, Alice read the leaflet as soon as she got home. Much to her relief, the leaflet seemed to have been written about her. Filled with a surge of hope, she booked an appointment with her GP to discuss the condition and ask for a referral. Alice felt jittery with nerves when she settled herself into the chair in her GP's office. What if her GP rejected her suggestion and refused to refer her?

'Hello. What can I *not* help you with today?' Her GP fidgeted with a paper clip while speaking.

'Erm, when I was at physio last, one of the therapists said that she has a client with my symptoms?' Alice was embarrassed to hear her voice tremble. She was a wobbly anxiety ridden mess and this was projected in her voice instead of the measured tones of pure reasonableness she would have preferred to be speaking in.

'Refresh my memory on which symptoms you mean.' Her GP opened the leaflet Alice had handed over and looked at it while Alice dutifully recited the same symptoms she had reported several times already in the months since the accident.

'Odd that you should mention these very symptoms as only yesterday I read an article which claimed that Fibromyalgia could be triggered by physical trauma. If you are in agreement, I would like to refer you to a specialist in this field.'

Alice agreed that she was, indeed, in agreement.

Two months later, after a consultation with the rheumatologist including various blood tests and x-rays, Alice was diagnosed with Fibromyalgia, by a process of elimination of other nasty conditions such as Lupus and

Rheumatoid arthritis.

'Fibromyalgia is a chronic but non terminal illness.' The consultant informed her in a satisfied tone.

'What's that mean?' Alice said with a tremble in her voice.

'This condition can usually be controlled with non steroidal anti inflammatory painkillers, exercise and a healthy diet. You will go through phases with this disorder where sometimes you will experience more pain than others. You may find that certain things make the pain worse.'

'Such as?'

'I know of people who have identified things such as alcohol, caffeine or stress and have been pain free for a number of years. That is not to say that avoiding these will work for you, however it is worth exploring this avenue. I won't need to see you again as your GP can prescribe your repeat pain medication for you. I would recommend that you contact this Fibromyalgia organization for advice and support. They are well established and as the national charity, able to answer any questions that may well come up in the future.' With that the consultant handed Alice a URL for the website, asked if she had any further questions and stood up to escort her from the office when she numbly shook her head.

Twenty nine

Six months after the accident Fern decided it was time for her to go back to Nepal. She felt torn between her daughter and husband but could see that Alice was gaining confidence and becoming independent once again, which gave her the strength to make the decision to head home to Gary. Alice put on a brave face when her mother got in the taxi which would take her to the airport, holding her fear of being left alone tightly inside her. For days after, the panic made Alice feel as if she couldn't breathe without pain. She couldn't imagine how she would cope without her mother's presence, support, love, and good examples of inner strength. Alice was blind to the fact that all of this was still in existence albeit at a distance and she wept herself into a raw, gaping wound of abject misery over the next few weeks. Worried that she would make her parents feel guilty, she masked her distress when she responded to their emails, instead sending long sagas of her physiotherapist torturing her, detailed descriptions of whichever movie she'd been to recently, what Mr Desderman and his dog had been up to and any other amusing anecdotes she could recount. These diversions also served to help her regain perspective and appreciate what support she still had although she knew that she was sliding towards depression faster than the diversions could help her clamber back.

A few of her 'pre-wheelchair' friends continued to visit after her mum went but left with distinct looks of relief when Alice declined their offers to stay overnight or to help in any other way. Alice wasn't surprised that they didn't protest, she had come to the realisation that she was a different person since her accident and that her friends wanted her to be the same Alice as before. She had become a bit of a recluse, due in part to the fact that she felt that she had nothing to make effortless conversation about any longer. *After all*, she thought to herself, *which of them wants to hear me speak, yet again, about my painful travel to health? Only Stephen, my parents and Mr Desderman...* Alice felt that there was nothing and no one else she had to construct conversations with. She also suspected that a few of her pre-wheel chair friends felt she was a self pitying hypochondriac and so she allowed them to drift away on the waves of her discontent. Alice had since made a few acquaintances through some local fibromyalgia support groups but none of them had developed into friendship yet. When the phone rang, she answered out of habit rather than any desire to converse and then realised it had been a few days since she had spoken out loud to anyone.

'Hello...' her voice sounded confused, unsteady, a fragile echo of its former cadence.

'Hello mate! I'm working in sunny Spain this week, can't complain! How's you been?'

Alice began weeping.

Stephen was horrified to hear her distress and he promised to come and see her when he arrived back the very next weekend. Not feeling like venturing out if she could avoid it, Alice invited him to the house for the first time.

The spark that she felt when he came into the room felt shocking, almost painful. She didn't want to feel a spark, she wanted to feel like the lonely, damaged, almost barren, bag of dust that she had decided she was. She mentioned none of this to Stephen, they were friends and nothing more Alice reminded herself. The afternoon passed in a pleasant haze of banter and Alice forgot for moments at a time that her mum was gone and she was going to have to cope on her own. Then Alice would force herself to focus on the reality of her life without her mum in the house constantly ready to give support.

That evening after Stephen left she wept with frustration over her body's mockery of the emotional grief she still felt over her mum's departure, until the absurdity of her behaviour made her smirk. There she was, feeling a spark of life, for the first time since her mum left and she was sulking about it. Squaring her shoulders and resolving to enjoy the life she'd been given made her feel a little better almost instantly.

Thirty

Alice continued to feel a spark whenever Stephen was visiting and eventually she felt so infused with lust when he was near that she worried that the glow would be obvious. Stephen began to visit Alice as frequently as he could. He told her he wanted to be with her more often but couldn't as he travelled so much with work. Alice tried to spend virtual time with Stephen by watching the rally Stephen's team was competing in, if it was televised. It wasn't her kind of thing at all, too noisy, crowded and hectic but well worth watching for the occasional glimpse of Stephen working at the speed of light with the rest of the team whenever the rally car pulled into the pit.

Eventually they got used to the pattern of Stephen's visits and found a rhythm that suited them both. He always let Alice know before he turned up in case she had made other plans, and Alice, if she had, always cancelled them. One of her favourite memories was of the first time they had made love a little over two years after they first met. Stephen arrived for one of their usual food feasts, carrying a take away and a bottle of wine. Alice felt herself sparkling (a light application of her glitter infused moisturizer added to the overall outward effect) and she could see that his eyes softened at the sight of her. By the time they had their fill of both food and drink, the hour was late and Alice was reluctant to part company so she invited Stephen to stay the night.

'Ah that would be lovely, the couch is long enough and if you've got a blanket for me, I'll be snug as a bug in a rug!' he grinned at Alice, flopped full length on the couch and pretended to snore.

'Ummmm... I thought you might like to share my bed...?' Alice said casting her eyes in the direction of her room and deliberately not mentioning the word sleep.

Stephen whooped with delight, 'I thought you'd never offer!' and scooping her up in his arms, he carried her over the threshold of her bedroom and gently laid her on the mattress. Stephen then proceeded to make love to her with such skill that she was left satisfied and simultaneously yearning for more. Alice took great pleasure in doing everything she knew to make sure Stephen felt the same way.

Their lovemaking extended beyond mere physical intimacy. The connection they both felt was electric and they desired nothing more than to please each other. Their passion for each other still burned as fiercely now and Alice had taken to having erotic magazines delivered so that they could discover and then experiment with new methods of enhancing their pleasure. Their relationship was enhanced by their lovemaking but it was the totality of their relationship itself which meant everything to them. They spent hours discussing their feelings for each other, dislikes, likes, desires, and dreams for the future until Alice felt she knew everything it was possible to know about another human being. Stephen knew she didn't. And, this knowledge made him hate himself. His fear of losing everything kept him from telling Alice his deepest secret. His love for her kept him coming back to her like a bear risking the wrath of a hive full of bees when it gorges itself on stolen honey. What Stephen didn't know was if either he or his little bee named Alice could survive this relationship without emotional injury. He suspected not but was so blinded by the fear of loss that he was incapable of doing anything proactive and instead dared to hope it would all work out by some kind of magic. Denial became an uncomfortable but constant companion.

Thirty one

'C'ya in a week or so love,' Stephen leaned down to kiss Alice's face.

She murmured, 'Safe trip my darling,' and was asleep again before she had finished rolling over to his side of the bed. She was used to Stephen's erratic work schedule now and had no trouble falling back to sleep once he'd left.

Stephen paused outside the front door, waiting for it to click closed. As always, without Alice, he felt lethargic, emotionally flat. Lack of sleep and having to leave Alice's warmth always had the same affect. The way this lingered tainted his behaviour and brought out the worst in him when it came to Jennie. He blamed her for the fact that he was trapped in a loveless marriage.

When Alice had first contacted him, he'd been so relieved to hear she did not blame him for the accident. He knew that he was responsible for the accident in part due to his fuzzy hungover brain keeping from being as alert as he should have been. He struggled to believe that he had been over the limit even though that was what the blood tests had shown but knew that he'd learnt his lesson. That was the story of his life, he thought. Whenever something went wrong he somehow always ended up taking the blame but this time was deservedly so. He thought he'd managed to escape all that that when he'd decided to never speak to his parents again and back then he thought that bad luck liked to follow him like the stink on a skunk. Now he wondered if he'd always made his own bad luck.

The letters from Alice had been a welcome diversion from the relentless boredom of being banged up. The one from her mother was less welcome but he felt it equally important to respond and attempt to make amends in some way. Stephen wasn't convinced that he'd managed to convey his remorse adequately and didn't dare hope that Alice's parents would accept his apology. He began to look forward to getting each new letter from Alice and started to take his time over his replies. Soon he was writing about things he had told no one

119

else instead of just filling pages with the biro equivalent of jovial white noise. The time he spent reading and then re-reading her letters had begun to fill a hole inside him, instead of being just a pleasant way to pass his spare time. When he got out of prison, he began to meet her for coffee occasionally. It made him uncomfortable to see her struggling with her wheelchair but she fiercely refused any offers of help. Worried lest his obvious discomfort should cause her to think less of him, Stephen soon learned to act as if the wheelchair didn't exist. It wasn't until he experienced Alice's distress over her mother going back to Nepal that he realised that he was in love with her. Not in an "I pity you and want to take care of you" kind of way. This was a "can't breathe easily when I am not near you" sort of adoration and it rocked his world on its axis. He felt exhilarated and edgy at the same time, as if he was treading on eggshells but relishing the crunch it made.

Stephen told no one of his feelings for her, not Simon, Sue, or even Alice herself, till much later. Simon and Sue thought he went to visit Alice out of a sense of obligation. To pay back a debit for the damage he'd caused. The realities of his feelings for Alice were too complex and tender to air in front of others and he didn't bother to try and explain the truth to them. Then they set him up with Jennie, Stephen reluctantly went along, wishing Jennie was Alice and began to drink to smooth the rough edges of the evening. Predictably the drink washed away whatever logistical insight he possessed about his feelings for Alice that he had when sober. One drunken night led to another and all of a sudden he was in an uncomfortable relationship with a woman he didn't love and not in a "proper" relationship with the one he did.

Determined to do things right for once in his life, he went to Alice first and told her how he felt about her. As she welcomed him into her arms he felt at peace for the first time since early childhood. He went straight from Alice's to complete the final leg of the European Rally. As soon as he got back he phoned Jennie to see if it would be all right for him to call round and explain "something" to her. He felt like a nervous schoolboy as he rang Jennie's doorbell. She had sounded delighted when he had asked if he could come round and told him she had something special to share with him too. Determined to explain that their one night stand should have gone no further as soon as she opened the door, he rang the bell, took a deep breath and squared his shoulders.

Jennie flung the door open shrieking, 'Looky, looky!' and waving a white stick around.

'Wuh?' Stephen braced himself against the door with a hand, feeling as if the wind had been knocked out of him. *Surely that wasn't...nah couldn't be...*

'I'm pregnant!' Jennie shrieked! 'It must have happened that night we had together when we were so drunk and the condom split! How special, how romantic, this baby was meant to...' Jennie's happy burbling trailed to a halt as she noticed that Stephen looked underwhelmed by her marvellous news.

'You don't want a baby? I thought you said that you longed for a son?' Her face crumpled.

Reacting to her distress Stephen blurted, 'I did and I do, it's just the shock, we hardly know each other, I...'

Stephen felt his newfound peace shatter into a million shinning fragile crystals. As he stepped over them to take the mother of his child into his arms, his spirit sunk as his mind's eye watched the crystals turn to dust. He proposed to Jennie, of course. It was the right thing to do for his babe in the making; every child should have rapid access to a father's love. He was determined not to follow in his parents' footsteps; he would be a great father and would do anything he had to, to make sure his child knew how much he loved it. Selfishly, Stephen tried to do the right thing for himself as well by maintaining his relationship with Alice. He may have married Jennie in the registry office but he knew he was married to Alice in his soul.

Now, a year later, he was torn between love for Marcel, the importance of child's need for a father's presence and his love for Alice. He loathed himself for being so unkind to

Jennie, he knew she did not deserve to be treated in the way that he did but he could see no way out of his predicament and like all trapped animals he lashed out at what he regarded as his captor. He resigned himself to the fact that he would have to wait until Marcel was old enough to decide who he would like to live with. Until then he knew he had to stay with Jennie so that she did not have a chance to turn Marcel against him. Stephen scrubbed his face with his hands as he thought about what a shit pit he had dug for himself yet again, the only difference was that this one had a couple of comfort zones named Alice and Marcel.

Thirty two

Alice squeezed her eyes shut, pressed her crossed fingers hard onto her thighs and counted to sixty slowly before she allowed herself to squint through one eye only, at the results window on the pregnancy test. A very faint pink showed, so pale that she could only just make it out. *Well what does that mean? Am I pregnant or not?* Alice wondered. A glimmer of hope swelled in her chest. She'd not say anything to Stephen just yet, he wasn't due home for several days so she would wait a couple more and then use the extra test that came in the package.

The wait for the next testing day seemed to go on forever. Finally two days later, when she was a full three weeks overdue, she performed the magical seeming ritual of weeing in an old jar and dipping the end of the tester in the fluid. Eyes squeezed shut, fingers pressed hard against her thigh; she counted again and then peeked. A dark rosy hued circle beamed at her from the white plastic.

'Hello baby...' she whispered, eyes huge as she stared at the circle before gently placing the test wand on a wad of kitchen towels as if to cradle it from the hard counter top.

Desperate to shout her news to the world or even just her street, she knew it would be wrong to not have Stephen be the second to know. She decided that she would tell no one until he came home and she had a chance to share their good news with him, she wanted to see the expression of delight on his face when she told him. That day Alice felt wrapped in warmth, suspended almost, like the feeling she always got when she knew she'd found the perfect Christmas present for someone she loved and couldn't wait to see the recipient to open it. Alice spent the morning feeling as if her world was wrapped in cotton wool, all the sharp edges were masked and even the floor felt cushioned beneath her feet as she went to answer the door. She opened it to see Mr Desderman smiling at her.

'Hello Alice, I popped round to see how you were. You look wonderful!'

123

'Thanks. I am feeling really well today.' Alice smiled softly and then was lost in thought for a perceptible second before she asked, 'Would you like a cup of tea?'

Mr Desderman stayed long enough to have not one but two cups of tea. Alice felt that her secret heightened her senses and she enjoyed his company more than ever before. He was a gentleman in every sense of the word, pulling her chair out for her and always treated her as if she was a fragile flower. He had a head full of his life stories which he recounted with great relish needing very little prompting. Alice thought he was looking at her a bit too intensely, as if he could sense she had a new soul inside her womb and she decided to deflect his interest by asking for one of his tales. He chose one from his boyhood which he had spent growing up on a dairy farm. Today he told her of searching for frog spawn along the riverbank. Once found, he had put some in a gallon jar along with some river water and weeds and watched those eggs develop into tadpoles. The words he spoke carried the spring warmth from all those years ago with them, Alice shivered inwardly finding a beautiful symbolism in this tale of eggs growing into developed independent beings. Superstitiously she placed a hand over where she imagined her womb to be, over the place where she got cramps when she had her period each month. *Are you listening to this story baby?* Alice thought trying to send her unspoken words down towards her belly. *Wouldn't it be lovely if Mr Desderman could take my baby to a river to look for frog spawn someday?* Alice imagined telling her child about this moment one day in the future and wondered if he or she would find it as special as she knew it to be.

Thirty three

Late the next morning she saw a smear of pink on the toilet paper and felt her stomach clench. No, it can't be possible after everything I've been through, Alice thought. In a panic she phoned her GP. She had to leave a message and waited anxiously until he returned her call. He told her this was not unusual in early pregnancy, offered her an appointment at 2pm and advised her to try not to worry till then. At 1:45pm Alice made her way into the GP surgery, worrying plenty but on a different level marvelling at the fact that she was able to move with more ease and stay out of her wheelchair longer, than she had a month ago. Alice didn't know if this improvement was due to the persistent physio helping at last or if it was just the fact that she was coming to terms with her Fibromyalgia and learning to overcome the challenges it posed. Alice was certain that knowing what she was battling against had helped her a great deal, even if only in her mind.

'Yes, definitely pregnant,' her GP said after testing the sample of urine he'd asked her to bring. 'So by my calculations that makes your due date sometime in November of this year!'

'So you don't think this bleeding is anything to worry about?' Alice said with a hopeful smile.

'Well, bleeding early in pregnancy isn't always bad news and you say it is brown now which isn't a worry. Much better to have brown than bright red loss down below,' he said gesturing in the general direction of her belly. 'However, I will refer you to the Early Pregnancy Unit for a scan though it will have to be Monday morning as they are not open on the weekends.'

'People don't usually bleed on weekends?' Alice's uncustomary sarcasm stemmed from her sensation of defeat at the thought of having to wait all weekend to be seen by the experts.

He made the phone referral, and Alice went on her way, still worried but looking forward to seeing her baby on the scan. Her GP had said that it would look more like a bean at this stage than a baby but Alice didn't mind in the slightest. The weekend passed in a haze of contentment, Stephen would be back the following week from his team building session which had been based in Italy. She'd only heard from him once while he'd been away, the mobile reception was poor and they were roughing it, sleeping in tents in the Italian foothills, doing lots of macho hill climbing and other bonding exercises. Alice didn't mind the lack of contact as it kept her from inadvertently giving anything away over the phone. Sunday evening Alice fell asleep with a smile on her face, the next day she was going to see the baby she had so far only dreamed of. Her dreams that night however, were, laced with tinges of anxiety.

The pain woke her in the middle of the night. Not pain in her belly as one would expect, this pain was in her shoulders. Relieved to have pain anywhere but her belly Alice lay there for a while with her hand warming the spot she imagined her womb to be until pressure from her bladder forced her from the warm cocoon of her feather duvet. Wincing at the pain in her shoulder, Alice wiped herself and moaned with fear as she saw the white tissue come away bright red.

'No, no, no, no, no....' she muttered to herself as she washed her hands and then dialled the doctor leaving her number and reason for calling with the answering service, who promised someone would call back soon.

Almost immediately the phone rang. Alice almost dropped it as she snatched it out of its cradle.

'Mrs Redwood?' The woman's gentle voice almost made Alice burst into tears of relief.

'Yes,' she said, not bothering to correct her on the inaccurate title.

'The answering service told me you are seven weeks pregnant, bleeding and having some pain in your shoulder?'

That did it, Alice began to weep, 'Yes... yes I am... my baby... do you think my baby is ok?'

'At the moment, I am more concerned about you, this shoulder pain needs investigating urgently and so I am going to call an ambulance to escort you to hospital. Can you please leave your door unlocked and pack some essentials like your toothbrush and a change of clothes. The sooner we know exactly what is going on, the better... for both of you,' she added almost as an afterthought.

'Okay...I'm scared...' Alice ended the phone call without the doctor asking if she had any questions and went to pack, fearing for her baby, pushing the shoulder pain to the back of her mind.

Worn out and in pain, she sat down in the front room to wait for the ambulance. She saw blue lights flashing and heard the sound of a racing bike engine not long after. A knock was followed by a pleasant face peering round the door.

'Hi, Mrs Redwood? I'm a rapid response paramedic. Your chariot is on its way. How are you feeling? Can I do some basic checks on you before the ambulance arrives?'

Alice nodded her consent and he took her blood pressure, temperature and stuck a clamp with a red light on her thumb.

'That's to measure your oxygen levels and count your heartbeats. We're all set now; do you think you can manage the walk to the ambulance when it gets here?'

'I'm not sure... I suffer with Fibromyalgia, sometimes have to use a wheelchair and I am in a lot of pain right now...' Alice faltered, reluctant to trouble the paramedic.

'Not to worry, my colleagues will have a chair for you and we'll get you up into the ambulance with no effort at all!' He grinned reassuringly and then asked if anyone was going to come with Alice to the hospital.

'Noooo,' Alice's tears spilled over and ran down her cheeks. 'My partner is away in Italy, he is part of the Toraldo Rally Team. He doesn't even know I'm pregnant yet, I only found out this week and he's been away. I don't even know if I will be able to get through to him on his mobile and there is no point scaring him when he is so far away.'

'Oh the Toraldo team? Fantastic bunch, their driver Gerry Holden is my favourite to win this year! Tora, Tora, Tora!' The paramedic's enthusiasm quickly died down as he noted the tears on Alice's face, clashing with his lapse into his favourite team's victory chant.

Another knock on the door announced the arrival of the ambulance team and a very worried Mr Desderman.

'Alice, sweetie what's happening? Are you okay?' He walked cautiously towards her as if she might shatter into a million pieces if he trod in the wrong spot.

'Hi Mr Desderman,' was all Alice managed before her tears welled up again.

He sat beside her on the couch before putting an arm around her, 'Need some company at the hospital pet?'

Alice nodded her head and sagged against his warmth for a moment until the ambulance team wheeled the stretcher in and lowered it before her. In pain and grateful for an opportunity to lie down, Alice sat down on it and didn't think to wonder why she wasn't being offered the chair that the paramedic had first suggested.

That was the last thing Alice was aware of until she woke up in a hospital bed. She felt someone smooth their thumb across her hand and looked in that direction. Mr Desderman sketched a smile with his lips but it did not meet his eyes.

'How you feeling sweetie?' His voice sounded tired.

'I don't know... sick, woozy... empty, sore! What happened?' Alice tried to slip her hand under the covers to try and touch her belly and felt something snag on the sheets, followed by a stinging pain inside of her wrist. She looked down and saw plastic tubing filled with what looked like blood taped to the stingy spot.

'Blood? Why? Is my baby ok?' Alice's voice rose higher with each question.

'You fainted in the ambulance, they couldn't bring you round, the doctor's just been in to check on you, said to buzz as soon as you woke and they would explain...' Mr Desderman's voice faded and he pressed the buzzer.

The doctor came and proceeded to destroy her dreams in a few careful sentences. He told her she had a ruptured tubal pregnancy, the shoulder pain had come from the bleeding in her abdomen and they had done emergency surgery to remove the bleeding tube, the only one she had left, and along with it her baby that had begun to grow inside it.

Alice had accepted that she would likely never experience the blessings and tribulations of pregnancy and birth but clung to the hope that someday they would be able to welcome a velvet skinned baby into their lives, perhaps through IVF or adoption. Occasionally she had succumbed to the lure of her imagination and felt her eyes prickle with tears of joy as she dreamed of hearing the words "I love you Mummy" for the first time. Her surprise pregnancy had been her dreams come true, a dream made of the most fragile spun sugar, impossible to sustain in the harshness of day to day reality.

In shock, Alice said to the doctor, the first words that came to her, 'It's just not fair,' and then she leaned against Mr Desderman and wept as if her heart was breaking. Which it wasn't, it had broken when they took her baby away, and she knew that was why she had felt empty. She was barren and she felt desolate, like a bag of skin and bones with no purpose. Now she knew the joys of pregnancy would never be her reality.

Part Three

Thirty four

Maggie Stowerby winced as she eased herself down onto her chair. Fifty two years old and feeling every day of it lately. Maggie wondered, not for the first time, if this would ever get any easier. Still, she agreed with the surgeon who declared her lucky to have escaped with only a fractured femur. What had she been thinking, chasing those boys at her age? Maggie thought they seemed hardly old enough to be shaving yet but their obvious youth and agility hadn't stopped her from giving chase as they sped on foot over the flat roof of the bin store in the East wing of the Barnstead Avenue Council Estate in late January last year. It would be more accurate to say she had been not thinking at all.

'Senior moment strikes again,' she chided herself.

Following them over the far edge, she had dropped down onto the rubbish and fallen thigh side down onto the edge of the cinder block wall before tumbling the remaining two metres. She had grunted with pain as she landed on the concrete below and frantically tried to grab hold of the top of the wall.

Laughing at the sight of her trying to pull herself up, before shrieking in pain and radioing for help, they had scampered away, shouting, 'That'll teach you PIG!' and leaving her to wait for back up to come and drive her home. On reflection, Maggie realized that she was lucky they ran off instead of circling back to torment her like so many tomcats on an injured mouse. She knew that she was fortunate to get back to work at all, let alone in just under twenty four weeks sick leave.

Maggie had gone half crazy while off work, first with the pain and later with boredom. She'd leapt at the chance to return to active duty, even though it came with the proviso that she remain desk bound, going over her paperwork from unsolved cases. Not that there were any free desks, what with the "Three Modern Ways of Working" being introduced throughout the stations across the country. *What a load of political nonsense*, she thought grimly. Might as well call it "The Culling" seeing as the three "WoW's" mostly involved making the already overstretched teams do more work with less people which inevitably was leading to more mistakes, more sick leave and more good police officers leaving to find new careers. The silly acronym made her want to spit each time she heard it. One of the three "WoW's" new initiatives was to introduce "hot desking", meaning less computer stations and therefore less desks, necessitating well developed skills in the sharing category. The remaining two "WoW's" were as asinine as the first and a great demonstration of what an underworked and overpaid bureaucrat could invent as a strategy to ensure a bulked out yearend bonus.

Needing room to spread her papers out, she'd appropriated the interview room and now could only hope that if it was needed, someone would be willing to help her carry her files out. Any leads gleaned from her paperwork would need to be passed onto another PC if further footwork was needed. That certainly wouldn't earn her any thanks from the recipient; as usual everyone seemed overloaded with work. Figuratively crossing her fingers, she grabbed the folder on top of the pile. Working from front to back, she skimmed through the details, refreshing her memory of the case.

A burglary: entry gained via back bedroom, with a substantial amount of household items stolen. One homeowner (Husband) not locatable and the second homeowner (Wife) finally traced to the local maternity hospital. Area of break in dusted for prints and wife provided hers for elimination. Wife claimed husband away with work and not contactable, wife left message on his phone telling him to come into station and provide prints for elimination purposes. A fairly standard burglary scene in the house and one case that was unlikely to ever be solved.

Maggie noted that she had asked for the prints to be run to see if anything matched, but had then gone and injured herself. Flicking to the next page she found the reports run on the elimination prints. Jennie Copeland's were clean, as she'd expected, she prided herself on the good instinct she

133

had developed about people over the years. A new mother would be hard pressed to hide anything, what with the temporary mental impairment caused by lack of sleep and excessive hormones. Maggie laughed, remembering her own struggles in those first few weeks of having a new baby sister to contend with. Mr Copeland's prints told an entirely different story. A history of minor offences, several cautions, hints that he was involved in more serious crimes but no firm evidence until finally he landed in jail but not before injuring himself and an innocent victim. Maggie blinked in perplexity, human nature never failed to amaze her. What did a seemingly sensible woman like Mrs Copeland see in a man like her husband? Perhaps she was wrong about Mrs Copeland, maybe she had a past which was well hidden? Reminding herself that her gut instinct told her Jennie was trustworthy; she had to accept that it was possible the woman didn't know about her husband's history. However Maggie did and she had a question that needed answering: exactly where had Mr Copeland been on the evening his house had been burgled?

Maggie braced her hands on the table and levered herself upright. After unkinking her muscles, she made her way to the internal phone that hung on the wall and pressed 0 for the switchboard operator. She then impatiently endured what felt like several minutes of ring tone, interrupted sporadically with the supposedly reassuring sentence "Your call is in a queue and will be answered soon." Maggie decided that the recorded voice was spoken in a monotone by someone who was either desperately bored or suffering depression laced with suicidal tendencies, perhaps a previous caller who had made the mistake of ringing to enquire about job opportunities.

Maggie sniggered just as the dead line went live and she finally heard a voice on the other end; 'Hi Switch, it's Maggie Stowerby, put me through to Lenny Hyant please.' She said and then sighed as Lenny's voicemail prompted her to leave a message.

'Lenny, hi it's Maggie. I'm back on desk duty only and

going over my unsolveds. I've come across some information in one of them that needs your magic fingers on the Council access only keyboard. I'm relying on you to track down the info I need to help unravel the remaining segments of this mystery.'

She left her contact numbers and ended the call. Maggie crossed her arms and sighed, first day back at work and already she had more questions than answers. There was nothing more frustrating than being taken off active duty Maggie thought and that was a fact.

Thirty five

Several months ago nothing could have convinced Jennie that she would be happy to be back at work. True, leaving Marcel at nursery was a bit of a wrench each day but part of that had to do with the guilty relief she felt at getting a chance to spend time doing something other than just being a mum. Once she stepped into the classroom she had no time to worry about Marcel and the satisfaction she got from seeing her pupils make progress, no matter how small, sometimes came close to equalling the pride she felt in Marcel's achievements. *It is a bit disconcerting to feel like this*, she thought to herself. Being a mother had definitely changed her. Before she had viewed her pupils as a challenge, now she felt a genuine desire to motivate them to make progress, and to work with their parents so that they too could participate in their learning.

Marcel, the little traitor, loved going to nursery. When Jennie had gone back to work in late June, she had half hoped for tearful clinging goodbyes but other than a few weeks of wide eyes and a wobbling bottom lip as she left, from her and him if the truth be told, he was now completely adjusted to the change in his routine. Marcel would happily start playing as soon as his bottom touched the floor and when he was helped by the nursery staff to wave bye to her, he barely looked up because he was so deeply engaged with banging his hand on the brightly coloured shape sorter. Much as she hated to admit it, going back to work was the best thing she could have done for both of them. She had gone from being an increasingly neurotic and morose mother back to the person with bags of self esteem that she used to be and Marcel had stopped being so fretful, demanding and anxious, much to her relief.

'So tell us Jennie... What has motherhood taught you?' Sheila raised an eyebrow over the rim her tea cup in the staff room.

Sheila, with her head of bouncy curls was the most gentle of Jennie's colleagues. She reminded her of an aging but well preserved Goldilocks. On the saggy couch next to Sheila sat Jon. He rolled his eyes at the question. He knew he could get away with it, he was the only male staff member and the women tolerated him like a kid brother.

'Is that all we are ever going to talk about anymore?' he moaned. 'I come here to escape from my clan at home, not to have philosophical discussions about parenting, the very thought of conversing about it tires me out!'

'Not our fault you couldn't stop sowing your oats at a more manageable number, whatever made you carry on after number four? Personally, I call that amount of kids instant birth control!' plump little Lonnie teased from the sink where she was meticulously washing a spoon before using it. She did this with everything, cups, utensils, and plates, anything that might touch her lips. She was the first to admit it was a wonder that there was enough time leftover to eat the amount required to maintain her girth.

'Actually, I think I will answer that question,' Jennie said hesitantly. 'Motherhood has taught me that I make a terrible stay at home mum!' She giggled unashamedly. 'I used to think it was outrageous when new mums rushed back to work early but now I understand why! I found it a bit soul destroying to have no contact with any adult for days at a time, plus it is very nice to be earning again, my savings were dwindling fast.'

'Speaking of other adults, how's that husband of yours?' Jon dropped the question in a desperate attempt to change the topic of conversation. Her husband's job made him long for the nerve to brave a career change. How he would love to work with a rally team furnished with a readymade excuse to be away for weeks at a time and earn decent money.

'He's fine, working away more than home lately it seems.' Jennie's flat tone indicated that line of questioning was closed. She looked at her watch. Shelia took that as an opportunity to turn and glare at Jon and Lonnie almost imperceptibly shook her head at him. Jon widened his eyes and mouthed 'okay' at them both as he thought, *Women! Honestly, some days it seems that they like to make a drama out of everything.*

The end of break bell rang and they all braced themselves for the afternoon shift of jollying new skills into worn out children's brains. With any luck all the parents would collect them on time at the end of the day; that would be a welcome change for the teachers and the children. It was a complete mystery how the parents of certain children managed to cope with their own children during the long days of summer with no teacher handy to child mind for them. Still they'd have to find a way, as the summer break was starting in the third week of July, less than two weeks from now.

Thirty six

The sound of a heartbeat wakes Alice every morning. Her own heart tells her it is coming from her baby but just for that millisecond before her mind wakes completely, and reminds her of the heart breaking truth.

It seemed that no matter how hard she tried she could not find her way back to the person she was before she lost her baby. It amazed her how close she had become to someone she had never met or even seen. The rage swept over her, a familiar sensation now. First her chest clenched, then her head felt as if it was swelling and the urge to release that pressure through any means possible began to pound through her veins. She had tried slamming doors, smashing crockery, shouting at Stephen, crying when Skyping her parents, all of it nothing more than a temporary release.

When Stephen discovered what Alice had endured while he had been away with work, he felt that he would never begin to make it up to her, as if their loss was somehow his fault. Above all Stephen felt confused. He wanted to grieve too, he felt most saddened by the fact that he had not been there to share Alice's joy over the positive pregnancy tests and angry with her for waiting to tell him. If she had told him then he too would have had that perfect memory to cling to like a drowning man who finds a flimsy bit of driftwood. The strength of his love for Alice and his guilt at not being there when she needed him most, kept him from shouting back when Alice raged at him. He began to build a relationship with Fern and Gary during this time, speaking to them on Skype with Alice at his side, their mutual loss helping to open avenues of conversation that before would have been impossible. Fern and Gary could see how tender Stephen was towards Alice, that he was there as often as possible to support her and try to work through their grief together. What Stephen told no one was that he had to push the loss of their baby to the back of his mind; he could not focus on that and help Alice through this. Stephen was sure that if he presented a strong brave front, Alice would begin to take strength from him and work through her grief.

'Darlin', you've got hardly any food in the house. Here, you get in the bath and I'll pop to the shops.' Stephen was glad of the excuse to make a few phone calls on his own.

'When I said I felt empty I didn't mean I felt hungry!' Alice grumped, deliberately misunderstanding Stephen. She grudgingly got in the bath, two months on from the miscarriage and still reluctant to take any steps towards being nice to herself. She knew she didn't deserve to be clean; a failure like her shouldn't have anything nice happen.

Outside in the fresh air of the early summer evening, Stephen swallowed in an attempt to clear the lump lodged there and without warning his eyes brimmed with tears. Grateful for the deepening twilight he walked towards the corner store looking at the ground and willing away the flood that threatened to spill down his cheeks. Calmer by the time he reached the local park, he went through the gate and sat on the bench. *Better get this over with* he thought grimly as he pulled out his phone. He called his boss first and begged a week's hols from him blaming 'problems at home' but neglecting to mention that actually he had two homes and double the amount of problems of a man in a traditional relationship.

Resenting the fact that needing to phone Jennie took him away from Alice when she needed him most, he dialled, already full of tension.

'Hi Jennie, how's things?'

'Oh pretty much the same as usual, part time teacher, part time mum, wondering when our boy's absent father will next be home…' She trailed off, leaving a pointed silence in the wake of her words.

'Yep that's it Jennie, straight in for the kill huh? You can hardly blame me for not being at home, someone's got to pay the bills.' Stephen felt his brain make that conscious shift that allowed him to keep his two worlds separate. He paused almost imperceptibly to adjust completely before continuing, 'Anyway how is it my fault that I have a job that takes me away? I don't hear you complaining when the bills get paid!'

'I'm sorry Stephen, what I should have said is that I worry about Marcel not getting to see you enough, but I suppose there are plenty of children whose dads are in the armed forces who survive lengthy separations eh? Never mind me, we'll muddle through somehow!' Jennie sighed as she told herself that it was no wonder Stephen didn't seem to want to be at home if she was on the attack five seconds into a phone conversation!

'Listen Jennie I have to cut this short as we are just about to fly out to Italy for some promotional work, I just wanted to let you know.' Was it Stephen's imagination or did he sound as guilty as fuck? 'Can I talk to Marcel please?'

'Ok… I 'spect he'll like that! Marcel, here, listen, it's daddy on the phone! Noooo mummy hold the phone, you just listen to daddy, say Dada, go on, say Daaaahdaaa!'

Marcel said nothing though Stephen could hear his breathing and that somehow was enough to make his chest swell and he knew he'd soon be near tears again. To distract himself he began to babble at Marcel.

'How's daddy's little man? You being a good boy for mummy? Make sure you eat up all that yummy food she makes you. Oh and here's a bit of advice from your old man… don't lick the cat!'

'Dada? Blabyagh, gruhh, bibble, ummm, uuumm, buha!' Marcel found his voice at last.

Stephen could hear Jennie saying, 'Good boy! What a clever boy!' in the background as if Marcel had climbed a mountain. Which, Stephen supposed, he had. Jennie claimed he said "Ma" when he was just a few months old but this was the first experience Stephen had of Marcel trying to engage in conversation with him. How desperately he wanted to be able to reach out and cuddle Marcel, to feel his weight against his chest, smell his soft baby hair. It wouldn't in anyway bring back the baby he'd lost, he knew that, but to feel Marcel fall asleep in his arms, to feel his sweet breath on his face would be such a healing balm. To be able to hold neither child at this moment was more than Stephen could bear.

On the other end Jennie could hear Stephen's voice break as he said, 'Daddy loves you little man!' and then the dead sound of a disconnected line. *Well,* she thought, *despite all of Stephen's shortcoming as a husband, he definitely loves his son* and for that she could forgive him most things.

'Travel safe,' she said into the dead space of the phone, for what it was worth as a good luck charm and then put her phone back in its cradle, high up on the shelf and out of Marcel's reach.

Stephen sobbed, alone, in the dark, on a bench in the park. *What has my life come to? This is crazy.* Internally he spat at himself, *Get it together man!* He wiped his fingers across his eyes and cheeks, dried them on his jeans and then used his hanky to clear his nose before getting to his feet. He knew that something was going to have to change eventually though, he couldn't see himself coping with this double life forever but that was an issue he'd have to concentrate on at a later date. Right now, Alice was at home, she needed him to take care of her and that he was determined to do so, starting with getting some food into her and then somehow getting her to keep the appointment with the bereavement counsellor the following morning.

Thirty seven

Alice held the card that they had been given by Mr Desderman and read the now familiar words. She had done this several times a day for weeks now; at first with a sense of anguish but now for the comfort they gave. A sense of the peace to come sometime in her future was lingering in the distance, not quite within her grasp but no longer seeming to be unobtainable.

The front of the card said:

Do not stand at my grave and weep
I am not there; I do not sleep.
I am a thousand winds that blow,
I am the softly falling snow,
I am the gentle showers of rain
I am the fields of ripening grain
I am in the morning hush
I am in the graceful rush,
Of beautiful birds circling flight,
I am the starshine of the night,
I am in the flowers that bloom,
I am in a quiet room,
I am in the birds that sing,
I am in each lovely thing,
Do not stand at my grave and cry,
I am not there; I did not die.
(Mary E Frye 1932)

The inside of the card said:
Dear Alice and Stephen,
I wish that I had a magic wand and could somehow take away your pain. I know that I cannot and that only time will help you come to terms with your great loss. I am here and want to help in any way you need me to. Please ask. With love from Art

Alice sighed. *Art.* It seemed strange to think of Mr Desderman by his first name. He had been a part of her life for so many years, great friends with her parents and now a comforting presence while they lived so far away and yet she had never addressed him as anything but formally. *Well I'm moving on with my life at long last and this will be another step towards embracing my future.* Alice paused in her thought process and changed track before she derailed. How she wished that Art would find another love to fill the space in his life that had been there since his wife died all those years ago. She wondered how he'd managed to cope with his loss. He probably hadn't had the advantage of intensive counselling like she'd had. Someday when the moment was right, she'd ask him. He was likely to have some wonderful coping mechanisms to pass on. *Oh!* Alice thought, furious with herself for being a pessimist, *Stop being morbid woman, now take a deep breath and another step forward.*

One of the biggest first steps forward had been allowing Stephen to talk her into attending that first counselling appointment. The counsellor, a warm woman of tiny stature and huge empathy, named Lilly, guided Alice and Stephen through their grieving process. She sat and observed silently as Alice cried and Stephen didn't. She paraphrased what Alice told her frequently.

'So Alice, you say that you feel as if the pain of losing your baby is similar to losing a part of your body. That it hurts. You feel a part of yourself is missing. How do you feel when you hear Alice say that Stephen?'

After a long silence in which Stephen's swallowing was audible, he said, 'It is simply inconceivable to me, no to both of us, that our baby simply does not exist anymore. Poof! Just like that, gone, taken away, without our permission!' He broke then and sobbed for long minutes in which Lilly first offered tissues to them both and then the opportunity to take the huge step of comforting each other in private while she went to prepare a pot of tea. Stephen was mortified with embarrassment over falling apart when he was supposed to be supporting Alice and said as much once Lilly had come back and he was able to calm himself with the familiar ritual of adding milk and sugar to his cup of tea till it tasted just right.

Lilly said, 'I have been told different reasons for similar behaviour from many men. Some won't acknowledge what has happened because they are afraid it will really hurt too much. Or that they feel that emotionally, they are not equipped to deal with it. Some men have said that they don't easily deal with their sadness and pain. Or like you, they believe that putting on a brave front will give their partner strength, when really what Alice needs is our compassion and empathy, as you do Stephen, from those around you.'

Alice said, 'I am struggling a lot with the knowledge that there is an expectation in society that making babies is a natural part of life. Therefore, losing a baby carries with it a feeling of failure. I feel angry that the doctor didn't send me in when I first told him I was bleeding even though I know that is was already too late for my baby but maybe if I had the surgery sooner, my last tube would have been saved?'

'Those are answers which neither I nor anyone else can give you. Doctors do follow very carefully set out procedures for any conceivable medical problem though I expect that isn't much of a comfort to you two right now. It would be natural to feel anger toward those who were in some way connected with or responsible for our loved one's death, it is part of the grieving process and talking about it is a step closer to moving forward.'

Several weeks had passed since Alice and Stephen had first met with Lilly. Alice felt that she had finally reached a place where the memories of her baby were mostly good ones and she comforted herself with the thought that her baby's soul had gone on growing after it had left her body and was happy and adjusted somewhere. Alice had finally broached the subject of depth of her relationship with Stephen to her parents when she'd told them of her miscarriage. She'd been unable to build up her nerve to do so before this but the loss of her baby had numbed her fears of their disappointment or disapproval of her embarking on a relationship with Stephen. Although they were able to accept that the accident had been a mistake, they were concerned by the fact that Alice had felt she needed to keep the relationship secret from them initially. However, they could see that Stephen was strongly supportive of Alice and that she adored him. In the end this was enough for them to accept the relationship and to say as much to both Stephen and Alice during a series of Skype conversations. Alice had begun using Skype regularly only recently even though her mother had set it up while she was caring for her after the accident, but Alice had come to realise that it was invaluable during times like these. No longer did she feel the need to protect her parents from her emotions as she had when her mother went back to Nepal. Now she allowed them to share them with her in an attempt to ease her burden.

Thirty eight

Stephen and Alice named their baby Alex. They chose Alex because they didn't know which gender it had been and thought that was a nice name and suitable for either a boy or girl. The decided to plant a Magnolia blossom tree in the bottom of their garden. Its limited flowering period would perfectly reflect and honour Alex's short life. Alice spent hours writing a poem of blessing for their baby. They placed it under the tree's roots with the hope that the words would make their way up through the tree. Alice imagined each blossom would cradle a few letters, offering them to the sun and the starry night skies. That her words of a mother's love would somehow become a part of the tree's beauty:

I am the cold dark Earth
That dreams of spring

I am all of Earth's love
For I bring the winter rest
That gives energy for
Spring's fertility, summer's birth

For even in the coldest
Darkest times

I am the child
Growing in a warm, dark womb

I am your life, as you are mine
Breath, pulse, soul
I am the life dance
Of which your spirit
Sings, cries, loves

I am sweet seduction
Burning lust, cold passion
Dormant, budding, blooming

Fertility

I am the living and the dying
That births continuous new beginnings
I am the cycle of eternity
Within and without you

Alice was certain that she would look at children in the future and think: *What would our Alex look like? What would our child be doing right now? If Alex had lived, he/she would be about that age...* Working through her grief had meant that her life had become a house with many rooms. Emotions that she could easily work through were the rooms that she kept open and spent most of her time in. Others, she kept locked most of the time. They held the emotions that she was working through, the most painful ones and the ones that might blow huge irreparable holes in her healing process if she didn't step slowly and cautiously. Lilly was helping her to open the doors and just stand for a few moments, and reassured her that she would eventually be able to enter these rooms too. Already Alice felt that it was okay to put their baby's soul to rest and no longer a betrayal or denial of Alex's brief existence.

Alice and Stephen agreed that Alex would always be a part of them through memory and from the beauty of the Magnolia tree. As she watched the petals fall from the tree for the first time Alice accepted that the difference between birth and death is negligible. That it was what you do with the gift of your life that can make all the difference to the world around you.

Thirty nine

Jennie grinned as she watched Marcel play. Her life was improving on a daily basis. She had been back to work for four hectic weeks before the summer school break had given her some time to concentrate on lesson planning for the school year ahead. On the marriage side of things there was good news too. Stephen had agreed to go to marriage counselling sessions with her. Jennie had begun to feel that there was some hope for their marriage and if the outcome of the counselling sessions proved differently at least she would know she had made every effort possible to build upon the ideals she held dear. If they came to the conclusion that they had no option but to separate, she wanted it to be as amicable as possible, for Marcel's sake. Her mother had sounded dubious when Jennie had phoned with what she considered the good news of the potential for improvement in their marriage.

'I don't understand why you insist on persisting with this sham of a marriage Jennie!'

'Mother! For all that you dislike Stephen, he is my husband, he is a great father to Marcel and for what it is worth I won't walk away until I can be sure there is nothing here worth salvaging. If there isn't then I want us to part amicably, it is important to me that Marcel grows up knowing his father. Uh sorry mum, I didn't mean that the way it sounded...' Jennie winced while she waited for her mum to speak.

'Sweetie, I hope this desire you have for a stable marriage isn't because your father and I split up when up were little?' Sabi swallowed audibly, something she always did when worried that she had upset someone.

'No mum, well maybe, I don't know but I am not consciously relating my marriage to the relationship you had with dad... If I did then I wouldn't expect Stephen to want to stay a part of Marcel's life if we separate! I still don't understand why dad wasn't interested in me but Stephen is so different mum, he adores Marcel. If you'd given him a chance you would have been able to see that for yourself but Stephen and you are each as bad as the other when it comes to having blinkers on about what endearing qualities both of you possess!' Exasperated now, Jennie began to pick the dead leaves off the plant near her phone cradle.

Sabi, sensing Jennie's rising temper, bit back the retort that came to mind about Stephen. Perhaps Jennie was right but Sabi was damned if she would admit it without an opportunity to see Stephen prove his worth as a father and husband. He'd been absent in both respects when she'd last visited.

'Okay Jennie, I am not so pig headed that I can't see that my distaste for your husband might have been obvious enough to keep him away when I was visiting. Perhaps next time, we can both make an effort to spend some time together and maybe improve our opinions of each other?' On that unexpectedly wonderful note they said their goodbyes and Jennie was left with the thrill of knowing that her mum was willing to get to know Stephen better.

Jennie had taken a day off from slogging through lesson planning, and the seemingly endless answering of questions on the reams of paper that were required to request extra funding for the children requiring additional help due to their special educational needs. Often the applications to the Local Education Authority got rejected unless the problems were considered "severe" as the schools received a certain amount of funding for this in the year's budget, but Jennie liked to have the forms ready for the beginning of the Autumn school term so that she could ask anyway. Jennie was certain that the picnic in the park with some of the women from the breast feeding group planned for today would be a much more enjoyable way to spend her time. It was already the tenth of August, where had the year gone? Jennie wondered. Even though most of them were no longer breastfeeding, it was nice to touch base occasionally. The mums all brought a dish to the picnic to be shared amongst the other adults. The food flavoured with sunshine and seasoned with friendly banter, tasted exquisite, in the way that food eaten outdoors

150

often did. Marcel, at the ripe old age of seven months was rapidly becoming Mr. Social Butterfly and happily playing with some of the other kids on blanket. Jennie was preoccupied with chatting to the other mums, pleasantly diverted by the antics of their assorted babies who sat or lay on a large blanket, circled by their mothers, who paid no attention to their own food and drink other than blindly reaching out for a handful of something or a drink. No wonder then that Jennie missed seeing the wasp climb in through the opening in the top of her can of soft drink.

'Jennie! Are you okay?' Bonnie laughed and patted her on the back until Jennie got her coughing under control.

Jennie nodded and wiped her mouth with a tissue.

'Whew, don't know what happened there!'

'Down the wrong pipe?'

'Maybe... I took a bite of a nacho topped with Wendy's salsa, my mouth was on fire so I took a big swig of my coke... I started coughing 'cos it felt like something scratched my throat...' Jennie shook her head and coughed a couple more times. *Shit,* Jennie thought, *that really does hurt, maybe something got stuck when I swallowed the food?*

'Can I have a drink of your water please?'

'Help yourself!' Bonnie said, handing Jennie the bottle.

Jennie sipped and swallowed until it felt like the lump was gone. Just in time too as she was starting to feel a bit bloated from the fluid sloshing round in her stomach.

Marcel started crying as another child on the same blanket grabbed the toy he was playing with and started chewing on it. His cries sounded as if they were floating around in the air for a while before reaching her ears.

'That's strange,' mumbled Jennie and reached out to take Marcel from Tina who had waded in to sort the battling babies out.

'Oh my fingers feel tingly, zappy, bit numb...' Jennie flicked the tips of her fingers against her thumbs.

'Pardon?' Bonnie looked perplexed. 'You're mumbling Jennie and, you're ever so pale and blotchy, are you feeling okay?'

Using all of her wandering concentration Jennie managed to say, 'Just a bit woozy, maybe it's a combination of the sun and something I ate.'

Too late, Jennie realized that she should have tried to describe the inexplicable feeling of impending doom that had descended over her psyche like a black cloud.

Suddenly, Jennie felt her bowls go loose. 'Here!' she said urgently as she handed Marcel, still crying, back to Tina.

'Jennie? Want someone to come with you?' Bonnie asked as she watched the young mum get to her feet and unsteadily make her way in the direction of the public toilets.

Jennie flapped her hand negatively in response as she gathered speed. The group silently watched as Jennie disappeared into the dark recess of the building.

After a minute Bonnie sighed and said, 'I'm going to see if she's all right!'

'Give us a shout, eh? This boy here wants to know when his mum's coming back!' Tina sat, back against a tree and tipped Marcel up over her head and blew raspberries at him in a successful attempt at distraction.

The smell of fresh shit assaulted Bonnie as soon as she stepped into the cool of the tiled room, rapidly followed by the sound of wheezing. 'Jennie? Have you got asthma? Need your inhaler?'

'No, I've had horrible diarrhoea and then I started breathing like this, I don't feel well,' she underlined her plight with this understatement and then went back to concentrating on getting enough air into her lungs to survive.

'I want to call an ambulance but my phone's in Holly's nappy bag…' Bonnie trailed off unsure if she should leave Jennie but knowing there was nothing she could do to help.

'Go!' *wheeze...*

Bonnie ran like she was on fire.

Forty

Bonnie ran without looking at where she was headed exactly, so intent was she on getting up as much speed as possible. When she saw a football roll past and heard a voice shout sorry, she realised that she was slightly off course. When she'd left their group to follow Jennie they had been sitting under the trees, the football game had been on the other side of the common. Bonnie lifted her head, spotted her group of friends, who were kneeling up, looking at her and clearly anxious. Bonnie veered over towards them, worried beyond belief, Jennie hadn't sounded well at all. *Why would the diarrhoea make her wheeze?* Bonnie wondered. *Is Holly still asleep in her pram?* She hoped so because she knew she couldn't cope with anything except getting an ambulance for Jennie at the moment.

'Jennie! Sick, wheeze!' Bonnie stood at the edge of the picnic blankets, looking at her friends and trying to catch her breath long enough to string together enough words to form a coherent sentence.

'Is she ok now?'

'Jennie's asthmatic?'

'No!' said Bonnie rummaging round in Holly's nappy bag. 'Need to phone an ambulance. Quick.'

'I'm going to check on Jennie.' Alison began running towards the toilets.

Marcel, who had been playing quietly with a teething chew toy, burst into loud wails. Tina scooped him up for a cuddle, looking anxiously at Bonnie as she checked for a signal before pressing 999 on her mobile.

'Go ahead caller. Which emergency service do you require?'

'Ambulance. I need an ambulance, quick!' Bonnie said, willing her heart to slow down to a normal rhythm so she could concentrate.

'You need an ambulance M'am?'

'Yes! No. I mean my friend does!'

'Caller, what is the address of the emergency?'

Bonnie gave it.

'Hold the line one moment please,' requested the operator.

Bonnie did as she was asked, making eye contact with Tina and trying to settle her breathing into a normal rhythm.

'Thank you. Please confirm the number you are calling from.'

Bonnie complied, '077567301.'

'Ok thank you, and what's the problem? Tell me exactly what's happened.'

'My friend started talking funny, then said she had to go to the toilet. I went to check on her and she had been having diarrhoea and I could hear her wheezing.' Bonnie turned her back in an attempt to shield Marcel from her words.

'I am going to ask some questions now. It won't delay the ambulance, ok?'

'Ok, please tell them to hurry.'

'The ambulance is on its way to you right now and should be with you in a few minutes. What's your friend's name and does she have any medical conditions that you know of?'

'Jennie Copeland. I don't know if she has any umm – what did you ask me?'

'Any conditions, any illnesses that she takes regular medicine for.'

'No, none that I know of. She has a baby!' Bonnie's voice broke.

'Ok. Jennie has a baby. Is the baby with you right now?'

'Yes, one of my other friends is looking after him.'

'Ok. Thank you for telling me this information. Is there anyone with Jennie right now?'

'Yes, someone has gone to check on her.'

'Can you ask her how Jennie is?'

'No! It's too far away. The toilets are on the other side of the common from where I am standing!'

'Please make your way over there now so you can tell me exactly how Jennie is feeling.'

Bonnie began moving, 'Ok, I'm walking there now. I can hear the sirens, is that the ambulance?'

154

'They are approaching your location. Please keep walking to the toilets and stay on the phone with me until they have reached you. When you can see the ambulance, signal your exact location to them by waving one of your arms in the air.'

Bonnie saw the ambulance round the corner, approaching on the road behind the toilets with its lights flashing urgently. She began to run towards it, one arm holding the mobile to her ear and one arm waving frantically at the ambulance. The vehicle pulled up onto the grass, cut its siren whoop off and parked close to the toilets with the blue lights still flashing.

Alison came out from the toilet screaming nonsense, 'Her arms are on the floor. I tried to get her to talk to me but she won't. I can't see her face, it's on her lap!'

The paramedics hustled into the toilet after asking Bonnie and Alison to remain outside. One paramedic climbed over the stall wall after he couldn't get a response from Jennie either. He lowered Jennie to the floor and pushed her under the door while his partner pulled on her ankles as it was impossible to stand her up so he could unlock and open the door. The paramedic on the other side of the toilet cubicle checked Jennie for signs of breathing and a heartbeat as his crewmate came though the now open cubicle door. Jennie had neither and he began cardiopulmonary procedures while his partner ran to the ambulance to get the defibrillator and oxygen and to call for backup from their colleagues and the police. Both knew that neither the oxygen or the defibrillator was likely to be effective if Jennie had stopped breathing more than a few minutes ago, which sounded likely from her colour and the information her friends had given. The paramedic came clumping back, heavily laden with equipment and his partner began to attempt to intubate Jennie. It was then that he noticed the swelling past her vocal cords.

'Frank. It looks like the cardiovascular collapse is due to anaphylaxis of some sort.' He cursed. Anaphylactic reactions had increased more than seven fold in the last decade and while they were never easy to completely resolve quickly, it looked like they might be too late to make any impact whatsoever on the damage already caused by Jennie's response to whatever had caused her to have this allergic reaction.

The other paramedic put down the defibrillator. He had been poised to place the paddles on Jennie's chest once his partner had got some oxygen into her lungs. Knowing this would be impossible if her trachea was that swollen, he instead sliced along the length of Jennie's trousers to give him easy access to inject the dose of adrenaline he'd drawn up into the syringe. They moved with great haste hoping to get some signs of life from Jennie, but it was too late, she was dead. The men transferred her body onto the stretcher, covered her head to toe with a blanket and wheeled her outside to the privacy of the waiting ambulance.

Bonnie shrieked 'Her son!?' and pointed to where the rest of the group stood as though they were pillars of salt; only the blissfully unaware babies showed any signs of life.

'Please keep the group together and care for her son until the police arrive. We won't leave before then as we'll need to keep the toilets from being used until the police arrive and can secure the scene. You'll all be asked to give a statement about the events that occurred here today.'

As he finished speaking they could hear the sirens of the police car. The back up ambulance arrived just as the paramedics were climbing out of the back of the ambulance where they had gently placed the stretcher bearing Jennie's body. The police found Stephen's number on Jennie's mobile and called to inform him of the situation but no one answered.

'Mr Copeland, this is the Southampton City Police. We need to make contact with you as a matter of urgency.' The PC left contact details and ended the call.

The back up ambulance took Tina, Alison, Bonnie and the babies to hospital where they were met by more police and the duty social worker. The police duly took preliminary statements from the distraught group and the social worker took Marcel.

Forty one

Maggie shook her head incredulously; some men had a lot of nerve! Lenny Hyant had come up with the dirt on Mr Copeland and very interesting it was too. Mr Copeland's name was registered on a second house at the other end of the county and after taking note of the years of birth on the register, she was willing to bet the woman's name that was also registered at that address was not a relative unless it was his cousin. A less cynical person might wonder if she was a lodger but Maggie had never been accused of being non-judgmental. In her defence, neither Mr Copeland nor Miss Redwood were trying to claim the single person's allowance offered on Council tax which had led Maggie to put two and two together and came up with three.

The strangest thing was that Mr Copeland had a conviction for dangerous driving which had involved serious injuries to a woman by the same name. Surely that was a strange coincidence and nothing more, but Maggie had become accustomed to life throwing up some pretty bizarre examples of human behaviour. One thing was fairly certain though, Mrs Copeland couldn't be aware of this second address. Otherwise wouldn't she have mentioned it on the night of the robbery as a possible place where Mr Copeland might be located? Which led Maggie to believe she was not aware of her husband's hideaway. *Well, he wouldn't be the first man to be caught living a double life, but it isn't my job to expose him, and as far as I'm concerned the case is closed and it's time to move onto more pressing cases*, Maggie thought.

Maggie was walking to the canteen for supper when her radio crackled to life asking her to report in.

She paused at the next phone in the corridor, 'PC Stowerby,' she said as reception answered.

'Maggie, Tony said to ask if you've got the Copeland's file with your unsolveds and if so can he have it on another matter? The computer records show that the file is flagged as being with you.'

'Sure do, I'll bring it to his office after I've had my tea

break.'

'Actually it's urgent, a child's involved, social services have him 'cos the father can't be contacted. Tony's hoping the old file can give some other contact details…'

'Funnily enough I have something that may help, can you let him know I'll be right up?' Maggie headed excitedly back to the desk she'd been using. Grabbing the file from the stack on her desk, she made her way up one flight of stairs to where Tony's office was based.

'So you think he might be playing away?' Tony leaned back in his chair and looked at Maggie under his raised eyebrows.

'Yes sir, makes sense, don't you agree? Now what's happened to Mrs Copeland, the baby's mum? In hospital having baby number two?'

'No, she won't be having anymore children this one, she died this afternoon.'

Shocked, Maggie said, 'Dead? How?'

'Allergic reaction the docs think but they won't know for sure until the post mortem. Found her in the public loo in Old Town's rose gardens. She'd been at a picnic with some other mums.'

'Poor little tyke on his own with a stranger.' Maggie's maternal instinct kicked into overdrive as she imagined how scared the little boy must be.

'I'll give the locals a shout, get them to send a car round to the property, see if they can find Mr Copeland.'

'See if they'll meet you halfway between their station and here. I want him escorted back; he won't be safe to drive once he's had this news.'

'Yes sir. I'll do the necessaries and then set off.' Maggie smiled grimly as she left Tony's office thinking, *it seems that Mr Copeland's pigeons have come home to roost, now he's going to have to learn firsthand what being a responsible adult involves, including being at the beck and call of a ringtone!*

Forty two

'Oh balls, I've left me moby in the car again, one of these times it's gonna get nicked!' Stephen said. He swallowed the rest of his tea and got up. 'Might as well make tracks m'darlin'. See you when I do!' He kissed Alice, hugged her hard enough to lift her feet off the carpet and then set her down with a smile.

'I'll miss you Stephen. We've been through so much together and somehow we keep getting stronger.'

'I'm looking forward to everything calming down for a while. I can't keep this pace up much longer without reaching burnout. I want to grow old with you!'

'Ah you say such lovely things Stephen!' Alice's eyes glistened.

Stephen took a deep calming breath, tipped an imaginary shot of whiskey down his throat for courage and said, 'The next time I'm home, we need to sit down and talk. There are some things I need to tell you, things that are important for you to know.'

Puzzled Alice said, 'Ooooh I am intrigued!' She kissed him twice more for luck, handed him his work kit and shoved him out the door. 'Travel safe but hurry home!'

Stephen walked towards his car which he'd had to park at the end of the road as there hadn't been any closer spaces, mentally spitting as he passed a PC and thinking how strange it was to see a pig in the neighbourhood. He stopped at his car and looked in the direction of the PC in time to see him pause by the orange blossom bush by his gate.

'Oi!'

The PC turned in his direction and raised an eyebrow.

'That's my gaff, you lookin' for me?'

'And who might you be sir?'

'Stephen Copeland.'

'If I could have a few minutes of your time sir…?'

'It will have to be here, I am late for work!' Stephen was damned if the PC thought he'd be invited into his home. Whatever business he had with Stephen it couldn't concern

Alice and the less she was troubled the better.

After the first few words emerged from the PC's mouth Stephen had to sit down. He opened his car door and sat on the seat, arms braced on his knees, head down. He was overwhelmed with mixed emotions. *Poor Jennie, what a fucking horrible way to die! Marcel must be terrified without either of us near, being on his own with strangers will be scary no matter how nice they are.* Stephen realised that there was no way he'd be able to protect Alice from the truth this time but brushed that worry aside to be dealt with later. First he needed to go rescue his little man. For the first time in his life, Stephen willingly and gratefully sank into the rear seat of a police car.

Forty three

Mid afternoon Alice heard the doorbell. *Hmmm, not expecting a parcel*, she thought. Puzzled she made her way to the door and looked out the peephole. *Stephen? What a lovely surprise but why is he ringing the bell? Daft man must have lost his keys*, Alice thought in the seconds it took her to unlock and open the door. Smiling into his eyes, it took Alice a millisecond to register that Stephen looked anxious and weary. A second later her eyes dropped to his chest and momentarily she puzzled over the familiar and yet unexpected shape that he held in his arms.

The shape cooed and then said, 'Bababab buuuuuuuh, phlib, dah, dah, daaaaaaa, bye - bye!'

'A baby, Stephen?'

'Remember I said there were some things that I needed to talk to you about?'

'He's not yours?!' Alice shrieked. She could not have been more astonished if Stephen had told her he was the king of a small country.

'Yes and I should have told you sooner,' he began and hugged Marcel closer as if to draw strength from his warmth.

'You knew before now that you had a baby? I can't believe this is happening,' Alice said. She could feel herself shaking, desperate to know and avoid the truth in equal measures.

Startled, sleepy and uncomfortable in his father's firm grip, Marcel began to cry.

Stephen had begun to reach out towards Alice but distracted by Marcel's confusion, he instead began to rock him, murmuring comforting words.

'This was no way to tell me Stephen, just turning up with him in your arms. Come back later and speak to me on your own. I need some answers and I want them today!' Alice tried to close the door and for the first time cursed the slow release hinge which thwarted her.

'Alice, please believe me, I have no one I can leave Marcel with. Please give me a chance to explain. Please? He'll be having a nap soon, can't we talk then?'

162

'Come in but keep him away from me. Stay in the spare room until you've settled him. Then we'll talk.'

Alice sat rigidly on the couch listening to Stephen making fatherly noises upstairs, to his baby squawking, to the sounds of their life that she had no part of. Eventually she heard Stephen coming down the stairs. She could smell his aftershave as he walked towards her but she refused to look at him.

'Alice.' Stephen's voice was barely audible.

Alice heard Stephen but refused to respond.

'Alice?' Stephen repeated, louder this time.

Alice fidgeted then reluctantly turned to look in Stephen's direction, crossing her arms defensively over her chest.

Alice sighed. 'Okay Stephen, let's hear the story of yours.'

Pulling up the ottoman he sat in front of her and looked up into her face. 'Back when we were still just friends, before we made love for that glorious first time, I was set up on a blind date with Marcel's mother, Jennie.'

Alice nodded her head cautiously, trying to ignore the sinking feeling in her gut.

'I was nervous, not that keen on being on a blind date... drank more than I should have. I don't remember how, try not to think about it in fact, but one thing led to another and we ended up having drunken sex. The condom split or got torn by a fingernail, I'm not sure, all I remember is that after, when I went to take it off, the business end was missing.'

Alice winced at the image his terminology conjured up in her mind. She felt unclean and desperately wanted to get in a hot bath and scrub herself until her memory was stripped of these images. Her Stephen, rutting like an animal with a stranger.

He reached his hand out to touch her knee, 'I was never intimate with her again after that.'

Hope flared inside Alice, a beacon of longing for this complicated mess to work out how she wanted, for there to be some way they could go back inside their happy bubble.

'I went out with her a few more times, I felt awful for having sex with her when I didn't care about her on any

163

level and felt that I could somehow make it up to her by trying to be a friend.'

Alice's eyes drifted off to examine the corner of the room, the far window, to look anywhere but at Stephen. Her knee twitched reflexively, effortlessly shedding Stephen's hand like a loathsome insect.

'You were seeing her during the time you made love with me?' Her voice sounded like it belonged to a much older woman.

'I was confused but beginning to suspect that I was in love with you. That first night we made love, when I poured out my heart to you, declared my love for you, that was and still is the honest truth. You are my world; I love you with every fibre of my being.' Alice felt his eyes land on her; she glanced his way and felt seared by his beseeching look. She forced herself to look away.

'No you don't. You have a child. No love is stronger than that.'

'Please don't twist my words Alice, a father's love for his child and a man's love for a woman are totally different and not mutually exclusive.'

Alice shrugged in response.

'I went to finish the last leg of the European rally the next day, remember?' Stephen sensed he was losing Alice. 'As soon as that was done, I went to Jennie to tell her that I wasn't in love with her, that I belonged to another woman, that I couldn't live without you!'

Jennie, thought Alice, feeling the tendrils of madness trying to wind their way through her mind. *Stephen and Jennie, sitting in a tree, K-I-S-S-I-N-G! Stoppit, stop, concentrate*, she ordered herself. Fortifying herself with a deep breath, grasping a shred of hope, she turned her head in Stephen's direction.

'Okay so what happened then? The relationship ended? How does Marcel fit into all of this?' Alice crossed her legs, then winced, thought better of that position, placed both feet flat on the floor as she sat up straight again. Sure enough, a bit of stress and her abdomen started punishing her too.

164

'Well what happened was… how I found out about Marcel was…' Stephen floundered in his haste to get this next part over with. He stood up. 'Jennie met me at the door with a positive pregnancy test!'

The sentence stayed between them, raw and glistening like the wound it was. With lightening speed, Alice puzzled through the possible reactions Stephen may have had to this news from that woman. He had always wanted a child; this was a rock solid fact. He wanted to prove that he was different from his own parents, that he could nurture a child. Unlike her, it seemed that this Jennie, this ripe woman, full of functioning baby making organs had been able to give him the object of his desire. Unlike her, a woman full of dust, barren and useless. Suddenly, with certainty she knew what Stephen had done next.

'You've been seeing her, living with her, don't tell me you've gone and fucking married her!' she cared not a jot that her voice displayed her anguish. She had no pride left after this betrayal.

He nodded and the motion sheared a tear from the track it had been making down his cheek and flung it to the floor, a shimmering reflection of what he had done to her trust.

Alice felt like crying for the loss she knew she was about to experience. 'Get out, go now and take that precious child with you. How dare you bring him to me, to taunt me with my failure to give you what you wanted most? Fuck off out of my life!' She shrieked 'Take him back to his slut of a mother!'

Stephen, desperate to remind Alice of his love for her, reached out to touch her cheek. Alice slapped his hand away, repulsed that he would touch her with the hand that had caressed another woman, even if only the once as he claimed. Not that she believed that for a minute, what woman would put up with a man who never touched her? Well she could have Stephen back, this mother of Marcel; Alice told herself she wanted nothing more to do with him. As she did, she fought back two pangs of regret for what might have been, a solid relationship and a stepson. If only

Marcel had been just a few years older and Alice had therefore not been betrayed by the man who had made her feel so loved.

Stephen moved about the house, gathering Marcel's necessities and then collected his sleeping son from the spare room. Clutching him to his chest and feeling the weight of Marcel's sleeping head pillowed on his shoulder, Stephen wished he was holding Alice in his arms as well.

He said, voice breaking, 'I'll call round some other time to collect my things?'

Alice spat, 'Give me the address of your love nest with Jennie, I'll post them!'

'Alice, darling, please!' desperation was obvious in Stephens's voice along with his determination to say two last things to Alice. 'It was NEVER a love nest and Jennie no longer lives there. She's dead!' Stephen wheeled round and with his back to Alice, began to heave with sobs as he left the house he had called home.

Alice locked the door behind him, willing herself not to look out through the peephole or the front window. If she saw them one more time she knew she would lose her resolve. The fact that she was glad to hear Jennie was dead only increased her self-loathing and the knowledge didn't take away the damage done by Stephen's betrayal. She turned and walked to the kitchen, pausing at the Welsh dresser to remove a bottle of cream liquor from it. Kettle on, she placed a tea bag in a cup and then poured enough alcohol on top that it floated off the bottom of the cup. She poured boiling water on top, squeezed the tea bag to get the dark tannin out and sipped its comforting heat until it was gone. Performing the same ritual again, she took this one into the bath and there she sipped and sobbed in alternate motions, releasing water as it cooled and adding hot until the sky turned dark and she could legitimately go to bed. The cats crawled in beside her and this started her off in floods of tears again. *Is this to be my fate?* Alice wondered. *To forever be a lonely woman growing old, with only my cats for company?*

166

Forty four

Arriving home Stephen decided that this day couldn't get any worse and once Marcel was settled in bed, he poured himself a generous whisky and picked up the phone. This morning he had rushed back to Alice's in a haze after collecting Marcel from the temporary foster carer. So in a few hours he would be AWOL from work which meant he had two calls to make and he decided that might as well get the most challenging one over with first.

He noticed that his hand was shaking as he flicked through the address book for her number but it was steadier as he lifted the phone to his ear after dialling the thirteen digits. *Lucky number thirteen*, he thought and braced himself for the inevitable onslaught which was to come.

Sabi screamed at the phone, 'You bastard! How come you live and my beautiful girl is gone? What have you done with my grandson? I hope you are taking better care of him than you ever did with Jennie!'

'I know you are upset but I don't think...' Stephen began.

'Upset? You have no idea. Don't you dare have her cremation before I get there!' Sabi threw the phone at the wall instead of disconnecting. Weeping, she blindly began throwing clothes into a suitcase. Sabi felt unable to think beyond going directly to the airport to buy a seat on the next available flight to England.

Stephen sighed and put the phone back in its cradle. *Well... that went well*, he thought humourlessly. Next he phoned his boss, Vern, to explain the situation and to beg some time off.

'Oh my deepest sympathies mate. Of course you can have some leave, how does eight days compassionate time off sound?'

Stephen vaguely noted that Vern's voice sounded uncomfortable. He pointlessly shrugged his shoulders before answering, as if Vern could see the gesture.

'Vern... um... y'ano... I've got my little man to get sorted and all, I'm a single dad now, huh? So, those eight days won't be enough. I've got the "monster in law" arriving on her broomstick, the funeral and everything to sort before I can get my head round how to make sure Marcel is sorted while I'm at work. So I was hoping you'd see your way to letting me have the rest of my hols all at once?'

Stephen waited through a few seconds of silence before saying, 'Vern?'

'I'll call you back!' Vern snapped before hanging back.

Stephen poured another whiskey and sat sipping it as the room grew dark, waiting and hoping that his boss was going to come round to his way of thinking. He was fucked otherwise, he needed his job but Marcel needed his dad at home for a while even more.

He snatched the phone up before the first ring had finished, 'Yup?'

Vern's voice said, 'Yup yourself! I've sorted the wife's bro to help out while you are off. Get yourself sorted in time to leave for the Targa Rally the first week of September!'

'Cheers!' Stephen hung up, relief washing over him in waves, mixing somewhere in his brain with the alcohol and causing tiny whirlpools.

'Nuf of that boozing,' he muttered aloud to the plant beside the phone. Looked like it had the mange, that plant, all stalks with only a few leaves on it. He felt the soil, bone dry. *Yet one more thing I'm going to have to add to my list of things to do, on the other hand maybe I could just chuck it in the garden and leave it to fend for itself?* He wished he could ask Alice, she knew about all things to do with plants. Sadness washed over him. *Stop*, he told himself, *think about things you can control, work 'fer instance!* The Targa Rally was held each year, usually in mid Sept in Newfoundland, Canada. So altogether he'd be expected to be away just over three weeks. *Hell, that was a long time to leave Marcel and who was going to look after him anyway? Sod it, maybe I'll ask the monster in law for help. She would no doubt be going back home after Jennie's funeral and I could offer to pay her travel across Canada from the Okanagan to Newfoundland.* Stephen felt himself drifting off to sleep as he tried to work his way through the myriad of things he needed to organise as a single father. Stephen woke, neck stiff from where he had fallen asleep in the chair, hand still clutched round his glass. He considered pouring another and then realised that he'd have to wake up early with Marcel so he got up and stumbled upstairs to sink gratefully into his bed instead.

Forty five

As soon as Sabi had closed the door to her hotel room, she phoned Stephen's mobile, not caring that it was 3am. It didn't even ring before an automated voice said, 'The phone you are calling is not available and may be switched off. Leave a message at the tone.'

'I'm in a hotel by the airport. I'm catching the red eye that leaves at 6 in the morning. Phone me back and leave a message telling me where Jennie is and the date and time of her cremation. I'd prefer if you didn't attend, I know you never loved her and it will sicken me to see you faking grief.' She pressed disconnect, turned her phone off and not wanting to risk damaging her mobile, she slammed her hand against the bedside table instead. She showered and then lay awake, staring at the ceiling in the dark. At the airport she'd been certain several times that it had all been a nasty joke as she had caught glimpses of women who looked just like her Jennie but each time she had looked closer, she'd realized her mistake. Each time her grief had blossomed anew in the pit of her soul, what would she do without her girl? Sabi felt that it was unbelievably incredibly wrong on every level imaginable for a parent to outlive her child.

She fell asleep to her memories of the glorious moments of Jennie's birth, feeling once again, the love that had been in that room. Brian had seemed so thrilled to be a father but it was a temporary joy, he soon made his escape as the realities of fatherhood, such as dirty nappies and baby vomit came to light. *Maybe that is why I disliked Stephen on sight,* she thought. At some visceral level he reminded her of Brian, wild and flighty; never to be fully tamed by the woman he had married. On the heels of this disturbing revelation Sabi fell asleep. She woke to the feel of rain blowing in through the open window above her bed. It felt like a blessing from Jennie and she drifted back off to sleep, her tears mixing with the raindrops on her cheeks, breathing deeply in an attempt to capture the smell of this most special rain forever inside her.

When the alarm woke her a short while later Sabi could see clear skies and she longed for the rain to return so that she could maintain the tenuous connection with Jennie. She turned her phone on and listened to the message from Stephen leaving directions to the mortuary, the date and time of Jennie's cremation and contact numbers.

At the end of the message he said, 'Please listen to what I have to say, it's important! I know you think I am a cad but I did love Jennie in my own way, she is the mother of my son, she'll always hold a special place in my heart for that reason. I know my behaviour at times didn't come across this way but I am telling you the truth, please believe me for Marcel's sake. I want to come to Jennie's cremation, I have already had a chance to say my goodbyes to Jennie but I need to be at the cremation in case Marcel asks me questions about it when he is older. Please allow me to be there...'

Sabi sighed; Stephen's tone of voice had struck her as honest. Perhaps he genuinely had loved Jennie in his own way, she was very, no she *had been* easy to love, Sabi thought, fresh tears streaking down her face. It would surely take the rest of her life to train her brain to think of Jennie in the past tense? She got out of bed and made her way into the bathroom. After using the toilet and washing her hands she began the arduous process of trying to get her contact lenses to stay in but her eyelids were still swollen from crying and eventually Sabi gave up. She put her glasses back on as she was far too short sighted to risk showering without corrective lenses, and stood under the shower for a long time, the steam fogging her glasses, mirroring the haze inside her body which she felt might consume her before the ordeal of Jennie's funeral was complete. After dressing, Sabi packed the few belongings she'd used and, with no desire to eat anything solid, she drank a cup of black coffee before making her way onto the shuttle bus which would take her to the airport. As she passed through passport control Sabi thought she glimpsed Jennie in one of the shops at the far end of the large waiting area. Her heart leaped. *I knew it was all a mistake*, she thought as she began to move in the

171

direction of the woman. Then the woman turned and Sabi realised that she had been mistaken. Her stomach felt heavy as stone and a lump rose in her throat. Sabi turned into the nearest shop and bought some more packets of tissues and a bottle of water, flights always dehydrated her and she was certain that if she cried any more she would shrivel up like a dried prune. *Yup, that's me*, she thought, *a dried up old prune, only difference is that all my sweetness was taken away when Jennie died.* Her eyes brimmed and she pressed her lips together firmly to keep the tears from spilling. Grimly, she made her way to her departure lounge, careful to chose a seat as far away from the other passengers as possible; someone trying to make small talk was the last thing she wanted. The crew arrived at the departure desk soon after Sabi sat down and she went to where they were to see if they would consider the idea that had come to her.

'Can I help you?' The clerk smiled in greeting.

'Hi. I hope so. Erm, I'm travelling to England because my daughter died.'

'Oh dear. I'm sorry to hear that.'

'Thank you. I wonder if it would be possible to have a seat in an empty row?'

'Oh. I am sorry but the plane is full. Would it help if I could arrange to change your seat so you are sat you next to others who are travelling on their own?'

'Well that would be better than nothing, as long as I'm not next to women in their thirties.' She paused before continuing. 'That's how old Jennie is, I mean *was*.' Sabi said then remembered to thank the clerk before returning to her seat in the waiting area.

Sabi was the first person to arrive at her seat on the plane. She sunk onto her window seat, grateful for an excuse to look away from whoever would soon sit beside her. She felt the air around her compress as someone sat beside her. Hearing a grunt she turned her head slightly in time to see an enormous man trying to reach the seat pocket in front of him. Hastily Sabi returned her gaze to the view out the window. *Dear Lord*, she thought, *if I didn't feel so wretched this moment would be almost laughable.* The flight passed slowly. Sabi tried to read but quickly gave up and spent time watching a comedy which held no meaning for her but it was a good way to avoid having to make conversation with the man beside her. When the movie finished and the flight crew began to serve meals, Sabi kept the headphones on under the pretence of listening to music during her meal. She had no appetite but forced herself to eat the cheese and crackers and offered the main course to the man mountain without speaking. Taking his cue from her, he smiled his thanks as he accepted her offer. When he heaved his bulk out into the aisle to use the toilet, Sabi took the opportunity to stretch her legs. She nodded at the slight man who had the aisle seat, having not seen him until this point. He stretched his lips into something approximating a grimace before sitting down again. Sabi wandered up her aisle and back down the other side rocking a little with the movement of the plane. She used the toilet before going back to her seat, hoping to be able to avoid having to ask the men sharing her row to move again during the flight. Settled back into her window seat, Sabi finished her water then tilted her seat back and closed her eyes, feigning sleep until she heard the man beside her begin to snore. She opened her eyes and watched the clouds pass for a while until she felt her eyelids closing. Taking her glasses off, Sabi tucked them into the pocket on the seat in front and then placed the pillow that the flight attendant had given her against the window and rested her head against it. Quickly she became chilled and shifted until she had wrapped the blanket around her before falling into and out of a light sleep for the rest of the flight. She didn't emerge from her protective doze until the cabin crew began to serve the light pre–landing meal. This time Sabi made herself eat it all along with two cups of strong coffee. She felt dazed, though she couldn't decide if it was due to the flight, lack of food or grief. It was a relief to land, she was beginning to feel trapped, and needed to get to her hotel room.

Forty six

The visit to the mortuary was shocking. Until she had seen Jennie's body with her own eyes the truth hadn't really hit home. Her girl was gone and all that was left were the memories they had shared. This gritty reality that was manifesting itself as Jennie lying so still, with her hands stretched unnaturally straight along her sides, scratched irreparably at, and then shattered, Sabi's fragile soul. At some level she accepted that it would heal with time, it had to, she couldn't continue to draw breath for long with this damage inside the core of her being, but knew that her joie de vivre would be left forever altered. She wanted to get the cremation over with, to see her grandson and go home.

The cremation had been a green one as per Jennie's wishes and one of which Sabi found herself approving. Sabi knew it was a bit odd to approve of your only child's choice of how to dispose of her remains but she felt that Jennie had left her with a message that Sabi's morals had been absorbed. It reinforced the fact that Jennie had thought of Sabi, in this respect at least, as a good role model. Sabi desperately hoped that Jennie had thought of her as a good mother. The gift of good parenting seemed so little to give in hindsight. Jennie's green funeral meant that all of her body had been donated for use as needed by people waiting for donor organs and the remains which were not required were placed in a cardboard coffin and cremated. Her will also stated that she wished for her ashes to be scattered in running water so that she "could be free".

Sabi hadn't spoken to Stephen at the cremation beyond asking when she could come to see Marcel. She felt bereft and knew he would warm away part of the chill that had settled deep into her bones. Holding him and listening to his baby babble was just the tonic she needed. Sabi felt honoured that he seemed to recognize her and allowed her to pick him up without a murmur of discontent.

'Ah he loves his gran, he does,' Stephen commented from his spot in the corner of the couch.

Touched by the generosity of Stephen's comment Sabi said, 'He is such a big boy now, grown so much in such a short time,' and then she silently marvelled at how he could sit himself up and lean forward into a wobbling "wanna be crawling" posture. 'When will I see you next?' she wondered aloud, voice forlorn.

'Actually I was trying to wait for the right moment to suggest this to you but now that you've mentioned it, I am coming to Newfoundland next month...'

'To Newfie? What for? What about this big boy here?' Sabi said, bouncing Marcel on her ankle, leg slung over her other knee which acted as the fulcrum point.

'The Targa Rally, it lasts 7 days and covers 2,200 kilometres across the eastern and central parts of Newfoundland. I've taken as much time off work as I can, Vern, my boss, wants me there the second week of September with the rest of the crew. I don't want to leave Marcel, don't want to leave him with a nanny and so I was hoping you'd be willing to come and spend some time with him while I work?'

Sabi was silent, shocked by his offer, torn by conflicting emotions of wishing to be near Marcel and loathing the idea of extended time in Stephen's company.

'I'll pay for your flights?' he added in case a sweetener was needed.

'Yes I would like to be able to spend some time with Marcel... but... I'm not sure our relationship would benefit from us spending too much time in each other's company? I have a friend who lives in St John's, so I could take you up on your offer to pay for my flights, internal airfare costs almost as much as an international flight and my low wage isn't up to it, I'll look after Marcel, with pleasure, while you're working and then in the evenings I'll leave you two and go stay with my friend.'

Stephen's shoulders dropped with relief, 'Thanks for this! I want Marcel to have as much time with you as possible and I'd like for us to try and get on for Marcel's sake, but I know it won't happen all at once as if by magic. This start is more that I dared hope for.'

'Agreed. Thanks for asking me to help with Marcel. I guess I should feel honoured by your choice after all the bad feelings between us, but I'm not sure I can go that far just yet!' Sabi held out her hand and offered Stephen a watery smile as he took it in his and gently shook it.

'Shame it had to come to this for us to start mendin' bridges. Want me to give you a lift to the airport?'

'No thanks. I need some time alone. See you both soon. Bye for now Stephen.' Sabi hugged Marcel, 'I'm going to show you some beautiful sights, sweet boy,' she said before handing him to his dad.

'Call us when you're home safe? I'll wire the money for your flights into your account so it's waiting for you.'

Sabi gave him her bank details as she waited for the taxi to take her back to the hotel, and surprised them both by giving him a quick hug before she left.

Part Four

Forty seven

'Thanks Lilly, my head always feels a bit lighter after talking to you. Shame about my heart!' Alice's laugh sounded false to her own ears but perhaps she'd managed to fool Lilly.

'I think you should be commended on your inner strength, your heart will feel lighter when you have come to a decision about what you are going to do with your emotions over what you call Stephen's betrayal.' Lilly looked at Alice, warming her with a smile.

'He did betray me but I'm not as angry with him about it anymore. I still miss him so much. I wonder what he's doing and how he's getting on with being a dad.' Alice's face fell, the light in her eyes dimmed.

'When you are ready you will need to make a decision about those feelings Alice.'

'What kind of decision?'

'Well a year has passed now and you need to consider whether you're going to forget about Stephen and Marcel and move on without them in your life or are you going to forgive Stephen and move on with them *in* your life?'

'Phuuuuuuh.' Alice blew her breath out and up towards her fringe. 'That's going to be difficult!'

'There is no need to rush, when you're ready to take this next step, we can talk more if you need to. Right now you just need to keep on having fun and maybe think about getting yourself a part time job; what sort of thing would you be interested in doing?'

'I think joining Liquid Rock has helped me the most besides being able to talk to you,' Alice's eyes brightened as she spoke.

Liquid Rock was a free style dance class that was held at the local pool, in the pool to be precise. Alice's physiotherapist had recommended it and she found the exercise easy to cope with because of the buoyancy of the water. As an added bonus trying to do the dance moves in water was often quite hilarious, so she definitely was able to tick the fun box that Lilly had suggested.

178

'Before my accident I was a PR rep for a club in the city. I have to admit I don't miss the stress of that job but it would be nice to get out and do something instead of lounging around at home.' *The money would be nice too* she thought. Without Stephen's help paying the bills she'd been dipping into her savings to make her disability living allowance stretch further, desperate to avoid asking her parents for financial help, although they tucked small amounts of money into cheery 'just because we're thinking of you' cards. True, she was permanently disabled but her mobility had improved to the extent that she did not need to use her wheelchair anymore.

'That which does not kill us makes us stronger!' she said ruefully.

'I couldn't agree more but I think some of us get more than our fair share of angst.' Lilly gave her a hug goodbye.

'See you next month Lilly.' Alice, swung her bag onto her shoulder, flung back her hair with a flick of her head and made her way out into the bright September sunshine.

She stopped in at the "Word to the Wise", the used bookstore with higgledy piggledy furniture and shelves stacked high with books. A counter at the back served coffee and cakes which the customer could take to a cosy seat and enjoy reading a book of their choice. Every time Alice was in here she felt almost sick with envy and wished she'd been clever enough to create a concept such as this treasure of a shop. She chose a slice of coffee cake with walnuts and a cup of dark chocolate roast with cream. Sliding into one side of her favourite love seat, she placed her cake and coffee on the side table, slipped off her shoes and reclined blissfully. She closed her eyes for a moment enjoying the luxury of the chair which encouraged semi recumbence in the classic Roman fashion. The lure of her book overrode the desire to remain with her eyes closed and she pulled it out of her handbag, opened it to the correct page and allowed her mind to step into a world pleasantly different from hers. As she read, Alice nibbled occasionally on bits of her cake that she reached out and pinched off without looking and sipped from

179

her coffee. Eventually her cake was eaten, crumbs ignored where they lay on her chest and the last dregs of her coffee cooled in thinning layers on the bottom of the cup. She felt the movement in the seat as someone sat on the other side, but wishing to remain in the world of her book, she did not look over.

'Psssst, you're covered in crumbs, cupcake.'

Alice grinned as she said without looking up, 'Hi Art! How was work?'

Mr Desderman had begun working as groundskeeper on a voluntary basis for the city museum. His duties seemed to have given him a new lease on life. He had substituted his suit and ties for soft trousers and thick cable knit jumpers. He looked years younger, as if he was in his early fifties instead of nearly sixty one.

'Work, as you mistakenly call it, is one of the finest things that has happened to me in the past few years!'

'Lilly was suggesting that I consider getting a job?'

'An excellent idea and I know just the place now that you mention it!'

'Really? Where?

'The museum is looking for someone to act as a guide for the coach tours.'

'Art, I don't think I am up to walking round the whole museum all day…'

'Nope, neither do I, but this would be guiding the people through the showcase section only.'

The showcase section featured local artists' work, everything from puppets to canvases to sculptures and changed on a monthly basis. It was something that Alice made a point of viewing regularly and the thought of proudly expounding on the talent it contained sent a surge of adrenaline through her.

'Oh Art, I would love to do it, do you think I have a chance of getting the job? What do I have to offer them that will make me stand out over anyone else?'

'Well you've got that infectious enthusiasm for local art and an ability to survive on the wages you'll get from working just a few hours a day. When I mentioned your qualities to the museum curator, he agreed to hold the job until I could ask you and get back to him.' Art wisely neglected to mention that the job had been advertised twice already and no one had shown an interest in the position.

Forty eight

Alice waved off the last coach load of pensioners; this lot had been from Penzance. "Pensioners from Penzance", the phrase suddenly struck her as laugh out loud funny. Alice had been working at the museum since September but not until now, near the end of June, had she felt that she was giving the role what it deserved. At first she had been quite shy and hesitant to expound on the exquisiteness of the art displayed before the visitors. Nowadays they were so absorbed in what she had to say that the coach drivers often came to chivvy them up out of the museum and back onto the bus.

Alice turned her back to the gate at the end of the drive and walked towards the gardens at the back of the museum. Perhaps Art would like to join her for supper in "Josie's Bistro", she fancied eating under the grapevine covered gazebo in the garden which had been nicknamed the "vineyard" by the regular patrons.

'Ah there you are!' Alice cried spotting Art winding sweet peas around lengths of hemp which he'd strung vertically along the fence. 'What do you say to an invitation to join me for supper in Josie's vineyard?'

Handing Alice a fragrant sprig of the multi coloured flowers, he said, 'I couldn't imagine a nicer way to enjoy my food!' and offered her his arm.

In the vineyard, surrounded by lush grapevine leaves and passion flowers, with the posy of sweet peas resting in a glass of water on the table, they ate, drank and chatted. Alice enjoyed butternut squash soup and goats cheese salad and Art snacked on olives while waiting for his beef wellington. They shared a bottle of wine made from Okanagan grown grapes called *The Kiss*. Each glorious mouthful begged her taste buds to savour another. They had drunk the whole bottle by the time they finished their meals.

'I really enjoyed that wine Art; the flavour was just incredible, almost like nectar but not sweet.'

'I agree but wine with a name like that should be shared

182

with a young man your own age not some old codger like me!'

'I'm not interested in dating anyone, your company suits me just fine!' Her face was set in the mask she wore when she lied. She forgot that he knew her as well as her own father.

He looked at her face and then darted his eyes over to look at the tiny grapes as he hastily blurted, 'Ever hear from Stephen?'

'No! He'd have some nerve to contact me after how he betrayed me!' The mask slipped a bit showing a wistful look softening the skin around her eyes. 'I miss him but can't work out in my head how I could ever trust him again,' her voice had started out strong but was faded to a whisper by the end of the sentence.

'Well I have been thinking on this quite a lot, Alice my girl. I've seen you go through so much in the past few years, and not once did you seem so dispirited and empty for this long, not until you showed Stephen the door out of your life.' He put his hand up to stop her from speaking as he saw her mouth drop open. 'Let me speak my mind and then if you want to disagree I'll listen to your argument, okay?' She nodded.

'I don't condone what Stephen did, nor do I pretend to understand his behaviour. However it is as plain as the nose on my face that you two shared a love that went beyond the ordinary. I do believe that kind of love can heal any transgression if allowed to work its magic, but it is you, not me, who has to believe in your shared love to get the magic flowing... and there's that baby to think of!' Art added almost as an afterthought. 'How would you feel if something happened that prevented you from ever having a chance to tell Stephen that you still love him, another tragedy but one that stopped you two from having an opportunity to attempt to make amends? Would you suffer regret? Consider these months without him a waste of your life? Alice, if your answer is yes to either of those questions then you need to make contact with him and see where you go from there.'

Alice, tears in her eyes, spoke after a long silence. 'I think I'd like another bottle of that wine... to take home with me... one to share with Stephen someday.'

Forty nine

When Stephen had had to arrange for Sabi to help with Marcel's childcare during the Canadian rally, he'd come to the realisation that he couldn't carry on working for Toraldo. The childcare implications were too complicated and Jennie's death had made him realise that he wanted more than ever to spend as much time as possible with Marcel. He knew he could hire a nanny to look after Marcel when he had to travel but Stephen felt unable to bear a lengthy separation from his son. Another option was to hire a nanny to travel with them but Stephen discarded this idea fairly rapidly. He couldn't afford an expense like that and even if he could, travelling around the world was no life for a child who needed stability and the security of a routine to grow both physically and emotionally. Stephen eventually decided on option three, which entailed giving his notice at Toraldo and finding a local job where he could use his skills. He soon found a job with a company that offered regular daytime hours as a mechanic and a place in a nursery close by for Marcel. His days were pleasantly hectic, comprised as they were of getting Marcel, himself and their lunches ready before dropping Marcel off at nursery on the way to work, then enjoying the camaraderie "in the office" before collecting him on his way home at night. Each morning when Marcel smiled at him and each night when he kissed his sleeping boy before making his way to his own room to fall gratefully into bed, he was reminded why giving up the big salary had been such a great idea. It wasn't ideal that Marcel had to spend all day in a nursery but so much better than the alternative of spending large chunks of his life with a live in nanny acting as a surrogate parent while his dad was away working. The fact that they had to eat generic food brands in order to make Stephen's income stretch to paying for the car and mortgage was something which Stephen quickly got used to, and Marcel was too young to care about anything so adult.

Simon and Sue had decided to move to Spain to open up a

jet ski business.

'You and the kiddie are welcome to join us mate. I'll give you a 50% share in the business,' Simon offered.

'What do I know about running a business, Si?'

'I'd run the front, Sue would do the books and you could repair the skis. It'd be a great life for the kid.'

'Marcel, Si, his name's Marcel.'

'Yeah mate, I know.'

'Use it ok?'

'No probs bruv, 'corse I will. So anyway what do ya think? Wanna run away to sunny Spain with us?'

In order to appease his old friend, Stephen drank some more beer and pretended to think for a bit even though he'd already made up his mind. Marcel had enough upheaval and change in his short life and Stephen craved stability too. Besides, England was where Alice lived. Stephen felt he couldn't move away without her, it would be like leaving a part of himself behind. As long as he stayed in the same place he could fool himself into thinking that someday she might come looking for him.

'No mate,' Stephen said at last, 'think I'll give it a miss.'

'Ok pal. The offer's always open huh? And, you'll come out for hols wont'cha?'

'Too right, as soon as I've got the pennies saved.' Which was going to be a long time, Stephen thought but neglected to say. He'd deal with breaking that news to Simon when he had to.

Stephen rarely thought of Jennie except on the occasions when Marcel would unexpectedly look or act almost exactly like her; when a certain quizzical expression passed over his face or when he fretted over something that Stephen would mentally dismiss as inconsequential. He tried to capture these occasions in a notebook so that he could share them with Marcel when he was older. He thought they might be important to him someday. Having spent a bit of time each day in Sabi's company when he was working in Canada, at first out of necessity when he had to pick up Marcel after work, and then out of choice by staying for an after work cup

186

of coffee before leaving with Marcel, Stephen realised that he could better than tolerate Sabi, she was in fact an okay person. Outrageously outspoken, yes, but in an intelligent, well thought out and amusing way, rather than deliberately offensive, which had been Stephen's opinion of her when he'd first known her. After he and Marcel had returned to England, Stephen began to use Skype to talk to Sabi once a month, using the video option, so that Marcel could try out his new words on her though sometimes he just did a lot of heavy breathing and staring at Sabi at which point Stephen would fill Sabi in on all of Marcel's accomplishments since the last phone call. Stephen made sure to tell as many amusing anecdotes as possible as he realised that if he could get Sabi laughing then she would carry on until tears began to leak out of her eyes which would set Marcel off until he did the same. *I guess I know where he gets that from*, Stephen would think as he watched them laughing.

Stephen had begun to sleep better, to dream of Alice less during the night, though his longing for her could still shock him with its intensity at odd moments during the day. Each time Marcel passed another milestone he would think of Alice and how she would love to be a part of the experience, each time he laughed at a joke he would, at some deep inner level, be analyzing whether Alice too would have enjoyed the punch line.

The day Alice phoned was locked in his memory as the day he admitted to himself that there truly was a part of him that Marcel's love could not reach. He felt his soul flex, stretching, reaching out to embrace that what it had, until now, silently missed. Alice made his soul sing.

Fifty

Stephen was so nervous, excited and everything in-between that his left leg shook when using the clutch as he drove to meet Alice. Almost overwhelmed by simple memories, of their coffee and lunch dates before he made his life complicated beyond belief, he drove up the lane and parked outside the stately home. Alice had suggested they meet for afternoon tea and he liked the promise of that, the very idea that she was willing to meet him for longer than just a quick cup of coffee. It was just two in the afternoon and he'd booked Marcel into nursery for an extra hour which meant he didn't have to pick him up until six that evening. Stephen's feet crunched across the shingle as he walked towards the opening that lead to the walled garden. Alice was at one of the tables that were dotted around the lawn. She rose smiling a greeting as he approached.

'Alice. Hello. I. Can I. I mean...' Stephen spluttered.

'Hello.' She flicked her hair over her shoulder. Her perfume, that same one she wore before, floated its scent of blackberries and warm hedgerows towards him on the wake of her nervous movement.

Overwhelmed with longing for what they'd once had Stephen blurted, 'I want to hug you. May I? Or am I going too fast? Tell me, make sure I don't do anything to ruin any chance I may have with you.'

She'd warned Stephen during the phone call that she wasn't sure where she wanted this meeting to lead. That she wanted to move one step at a time, including sideways if needed. Alice now responded by placing her arms around his neck and drawing him close. Stephen could feel her breath make its way through his shirt to his chest and the warmth of her body against his. All too soon the contact was over as Alice tensed then pulled away, gently. Stephen looked at Alice, confused. Using her eyes she indicated the people sat at the other tables.

'Oh.' Stephen laughed, relieved. 'I was in another world just then. Sorry. Felt lovely to hold you again though.' He moved to pull out a chair for Alice and they both laughed as he tried to slide it under her bottom as the chair feet caught against the grass. 'That's a bit more difficult than doing it on a smooth floor indoors!'

The waitress took their orders for tea and coffee. They'd agreed to start there and see how they felt about staying longer once they'd finished these drinks.

Once the waitress had delivered their drinks and Alice's tea had brewed to her satisfaction, she leaned forward and said, 'So Stephen, let's start from the beginning shall we?' Stephen nodded and looked quizzically at Alice. 'You go first,' she said. 'Tell me again how it all happened.'

Stephen explained, once again, how he'd met Jennie, how much or little, depending on the perspective used, Simon and Sue had known about her and why he'd come to make the decisions he had.

'You know, I always wondered why I never met Simon and Sue,' Alice said. 'I brought it up on several occasions, didn't I?' Stephen nodded. 'But, you were always rushing off to work and then we lost Alex and everything just kind of fell apart.' Alice's eyes brimmed and she looked down at the table, fighting for control.

'Darling.' That one word out of Stephen somehow managed to convey clearly his anguish at the grief he'd caused Alice and the loss of their child. 'I'm so sorry for the way I treated you. I behaved stupidly, immaturely, like a complete arse. No woman has ever meant to me what you do. Please.' Stephen's voice faltered. 'Please give me a chance to show you, to prove to you how much I love you.' His voice was just above a whisper by the time he'd finished but clearly audible due to their close proximity.

Alice recognised this tone. He'd always used it whenever he was at his most sincere, almost as if he expected to be automatically disbelieved.

She looked up and gave Stephen a watery smile, 'Let's start with something to eat shall we? See how we get on from there?'

They both ordered afternoon tea with champagne. It came

with two tiny bottles, no more than a glass each but that, along with numerous cups of tea, lubricated the rough edges of their initially awkward conversation and it moved towards something which began to resemble the smooth language of their love that they'd been used to.

From that wonderful day they went from strength to strength, meeting during Stephen's lunch breaks a few times a week and then venturing out in the evenings too. Stephen would call round Alice's to collect her. They invariably had a late start to the evenings as he preferred to put Marcel to bed before he went out instead of leaving the sitter, a girl from Marcel's nursery, to do it and Alice lived a forty-five minute drive away from Stephen. He explained to Alice that he didn't think it was fair for Marcel to be at pre-school all day and then be put to bed by someone other than Stephen which she agreed was perfectly reasonable.

Fifty one

The months passed with Stephen and Alice struggling to fit in enough time for each other around the demands of work, travel time between their respective cities and the time Marcel needed from Stephen.

'Do you think you're ready to meet Marcel yet sweetie?' Stephen asked without daring to really hope. Marcel had become increasingly curious about who his dad was going out to see in the evenings when Sally, one of the workers from his pre-school, came round to stay with him. Stephen had broached the subject several times now but Alice was obviously not keen, worried that their relationship would fall at this last hurdle.

'Yes. I need to but I am scared. What if he doesn't like me Stephen? What then?'

'Marcel is a kind, sweet child. He's asking to meet you. You're a kind, sweet woman. You want to get to know him better. I know I am biased about both of you but I can't imagine why he wouldn't like you.' Stephen gave her the same answer as every time before because it was the only answer he could give.

'Yes, ok, Stephen. When can I meet Marcel?' Alice said much to her and Stephen's surprise.

They agreed to have the first meeting between Alice and Marcel at Stephen's. An unexpected hurdle for Alice. Stephen had never sold the house because it suited his needs as a single dad, with its two bedrooms and close proximity to the park a few streets away, and a short drive to the city centre where Marcel's pre-school was located. Stephen worked in a garage ten minutes drive from there.

Alice dreaded walking into the house where Jennie had lived even though Stephen was quick to reassure her that he had removed, or stored away for Marcel to look at when he was older, everything that was distinctly Jennie.

Alice knocked on the door. Silence. A long silence. Then, the letterbox flap lifted and a quiet voice said, 'Daddy's doing a poo.' Alice laughed.

191

A somewhat flustered Stephen opened the door a few minutes later, backing away awkwardly so Alice could come in, 'Sorry. Nerves got the better of me. Marcel you're not s'posed to tell people waiting at the door *everything*, just say Daddy will be a minute.' He reached behind his legs and gently drew out the boy who had been hiding there. 'Marcel this is my friend Alice. Alice this is my big boy Marcel.'

Alice fell in love in that instant. Hard, serious, hungry, mummy, love. She had seen photos of him but they didn't capture the softness of him, the way he seemed to almost glow with vibrant life. Marcel was something special in his own right, he wasn't just Stephen and Jennie's child, and Alice knew that she wanted to be a part of his life.

A split second later she said, 'Hello Marcel, nice to meet you. Do you like colouring?' and she handed him a colouring book.

Marcel nodded, handed the book to his father and left the room. Alice looked a question at Stephen, feeling a prickle of tears at the back of her eyes.

'I expect he's gone for his crayons,' Stephen smiled and hugged her. Caught up in the moment he began to sing along to a song that was playing on the radio.

'I don't like this song!' Marcel had returned and was standing with crayons in hand, waiting for attention.

'Well don't listen to it then,' Stephen said.

'I have to. I can't close my ears you know,' said Marcel haughtily as he grabbed Alice's hand, 'want to do colouring with me?'

'Yes please, that'd be fun.'

Alice and Marcel coloured off and on throughout the afternoon. Every once in a while he'd drag Alice off to another part of the house to look at something; his fish, Loopy the mad cat, toys, art work, and they had to stop to watch his favourite children's show. Alice enjoyed it as much as Marcel, quickly picking up the theme tune and singing it lustily as the programme ended while Stephen sat and watched them, shaking his head in amusement. Underneath her frivolity Alice was greatly relieved that she wasn't finding it too difficult to be in the house that Stephen had shared with Jennie. She didn't think she would ever feel comfortable there but at least there were no visible traces of Jennie's home decorating choices, no framed photos with her in them.

She turned to Marcel, 'Would you like to come visit me at my house? I've got two cats and Mr Desderman, my neighbour, has a puppy.' Marcel shrieked with excitement, clapped his hands and nodded repeatedly.

Stephen laughed and said 'I think that's a yes!'

Several months later Alice turned to Stephen one evening and said, 'I think it's time we moved in together, don't you?'

'I thought you'd never ask!' Stephen grinned and pulled her close for a hug.

Alice relaxed into his arms for a moment before pulling away to punch him gently on the arm, 'You were waiting for me to ask?'

'I didn't want to rush you my love.'

'Oh.' Alice was silent a moment before saying, 'Should we sell both places and buy a new one somewhere else Stephen?'

'I wouldn't ask you to move away from Art, darling, I'd miss him too much m'self! Now that I've given up the grind of working for Toraldo I can get a job anywhere, mechanics will always be in demand y'ano? I've asked Marcel and he wants to move there, you know he doesn't like his school because they do PE "*all the time*". There's nothing to keep us here.'

Alice was hugely relieved to not have the burden of living in the same house that Stephen had shared with Jennie although she couldn't help but worry that uprooting Marcel to move to her house was a selfish expectation on her part.

Fifty two

In November, almost eighteen months after Alice's phone call, Stephen, Marcel and Loopy moved into Alice's house. Their house soon became a home filled with the music of laughter and the sounds of love. Almost three years had passed in what seemed the blink of an eye though Alice had got over the urge to rub her eyes in an attempt to test the reality of it all. For a while, each morning after she woke, Alice had expected it all to dissolve into nothing more than a dream. She knew it was real now; she had the wedding ring and family photos should she need further reassurance. Marcel was a lovely happy boy, he had started year four at school and was showing signs of real talent as a dancer even at this young age. Sabi said that Jennie had danced well too, top of her class and teacher's favourite to succeed until she suddenly lost interest for no reason she could ever define. Stephen had been less keen to acknowledge and encourage Marcel's natural skills but had bowed down to a combined onslaught of nagging from Sabi and Alice.

It should seem strange that they had become allies, Stephen thought, but he knew that the power of their love for Marcel had led them to accept and then enjoy each other's company. So much in fact, that Sabi had acted as second witness to their wedding, with Art as their first, while Alice's parents kept Marcel occupied during the ceremony. Alice's parents, Sabi and Art had worked this arrangement out themselves when Alice and Stephen had presented them with the options. A move which Alice and Stephen congratulated themselves on for their sheer cleverness as it allowed them to avoid making a decision which might inadvertently offend any of the four elders. Simon and Sue had come over from Spain with their daughter. Sue was pregnant again and glowing. The expat life clearly suited them all which was good, as although Alice was civil to them Stephen knew she'd never be willing to consider them her friends. Alice had a surprisingly stubborn side to her which Stephen had learned to appreciate and tolerate in equal measures. Sabi, however, had moved over to England permanently much to Marcel and Alice's delight. Grudgingly Stephen had to admit that he didn't actually mind Sabi's close proximity either, she was all right, he'd realized, once he'd taken the time to get to know her during all those Skype calls. Art had offered her the use of his spare room until she got settled and recovered from the culture shock. England might be her country of birth but she hadn't lived on this side of the water, as Art liked to call it, for a great number of years. Sabi had eagerly accepted Art's kind offer as it meant she would be a few houses down from Marcel and with the added bonus of being able to spend time in the company of someone her own age too. Months later she was still there and showed no signs of looking for another place to call home.

'Alice? Any idea when Sabi's going to get a place of her own?'

'No idea Stephen, I'm not sure she is going to, they seem quite comfortable together don't you think?'

'Why, that wiley old fox!' Stephen spent a moment in silent admiration.

'I say good on them, how lovely to find someone special, especially at their age.'

'Gives us younger blokes hope that's for sure! Heh, heh!'

'What on earth do you mean by that comment?'

'Well, I quite like the thought of... erm... playing indoor sports with you when we are in our 70's!'

'Hah! Ditto!' Alice giggled.

'Why is ditto funny? What's ditto?' Marcel pitched in from the kitchen where he'd been getting a drink.

Stephen chuckled to himself as he listened to Alice struggle to answer the question to Marcel's satisfaction. He wisely stayed out of the conversation; he had no hope of outsmarting his son, that boy was clever without a doubt. *Shame he's wasting his brains on dancing, I can't understand the attraction, seems a poofty sort of activity for a male in my opinion*, Stephen thought. Wisely, he had learned to not voice any comments of that nature within earshot of Alice or Sabi who verbally battered his ears

195

whenever he forgot, or Marcel who looked disdainfully at him and said, 'Why's it matter, I just like it that's all!' *That kind of comeback from a kid who would be only be nine years old in January?* Stephen knew that Marcel's intelligence didn't come from him, he'd always been more interested in rough and tumble activities.

'All right young man, enough chatter, it's time for you to have your bath or there will be no time for reading before bed.' Alice said firmly.

'I'm trying to get there. You were distracting me!'

'Yes. Very trying,' Stephen said with a smirk.

'Oh, har, har, very funny dad,' Marcel flounced out of the room.

'Stephen?'

'Uh oh. I know that tone of voice Alice. It's the one you use when you want to talk me into something.'

'You'd be right.' She paused.

'What woman? Let's have it. What grand plan have you been playing with in that clever mind of yours?'

'Your parents,' Alice began.

'Not this again. Please?'

'Stephen. I know you've got your reasons for stopping contact with them. They treated you badly, you didn't have the greatest childhood and you feel they kicked you out just because they found you too much hard work.'

'No. He mostly treated me bad. Sometimes he took me out for the day and we'd do fun things like racing homemade go-karts down the steepest grassy hills we could find. Once in a while he'd take me out on the back of his motorcycle while he did crazy stuff like going around roundabouts the wrong way, Christ knows how he didn't get arrested and I was usually just scared shitless instead of having fun but mostly he couldn't be bothered to make any effort with me. Mum was ok to me when she had the time to stop long enough but my dad always seemed to want all of her attention.'

'Oh Stephen, I can't imagine how awful that must have been for you. You never told me the motorcycling story before. But, darling, that was such a long time ago. Don't you want them to know what a success you are? That they have a beautiful grandson? You know Marcel's interested in them now.'

'Why? So my dad can treat him like shit too?' Stephen's voice hardened.

'No. We'd never allow that to happen. Marcel's only a boy sweetie, he doesn't understand the anger you feel over the way they treated you. I was thinking that maybe your dad has had long enough of a chance to regret his actions, that maybe they are missing you. You'll never know if you don't find out and, Stephen, this is what bothers me most, what if you leave it too long and then it is too late?' Alice left the unspoken words of death and the grief that almost always follows hanging in the air between them.

Stephen was silent for a while, staring at nothing as he thought, 'Yeah. Christ, the old man must be in his late fifties now, that's if he hasn't drunk his'self to death already and my mum'ud be in her early fifties. Hummmmm. I've still got their phone number y'ano? Maybe I'll try a phone call and hope mum answers.'

'Or a letter Stephen?'

'Yeah I like that idea better. Problem is I wouldn't know what to say really or where to start.'

'Start with hello.'

'Help me write it?'

'Of course I will.'

Marcel, hair still damp from his bath, wandered into the living room.

'Nite dad.' He leaned over and hugged him then planted a sloppy very wet kiss on his cheek and ran off laughing.

'Urgh ya little sod! When you least expect it, I'll be returning the favour! Remember, you gotta sleep sometime! Sweet dreams.'

'Oh Stephen!' Alice tutted. 'You'll give him nightmares.' She planted a kiss on top of Stephen's head and he returned the compliment by tilting his head sideways to kiss her hand before she followed Marcel from the room.

Climbing into bed Marcel said, 'Can you read to me

tonight please? Two stories?'

'You can read just fine by yourself! How about I read you one and you read me one?' They settled on the continuing saga about the adventures of a group of boys who formed a secret club. Alice kissed Marcel after tucking him in then said, 'Straight to sleep now, you've got an early Saturday dance class remember?'

'Yes indeedy!' Marcel snuggled down and grinned, looking up at her through half closed eyes, his long lashes nearly brushing his cheeks.

Alice leaned over, kissed him again and said, 'Night sweetheart, I love you all up.' Turning out his bedside light she walked towards the door.

'Mum?'

'Yes my beautiful boy?'

'I love you too, a hundred lots, you're the bestest!'

Alice's answering smile was radiant. *Maybe I am*, she thought, *maybe I am.*

Fifty three

Alice came downstairs and turned into the kitchen, 'I'm putting the kettle on, do you want a cuppa?' she called.

'I'm going to have a glass of wine, want one?' he responded. 'Oh and would you mind bringing some food back with you? I've put a plate of nibbles in the fridge.'

Alice could hear Stephen twisting the cork out of the bottle. That man would never master the hinge technique on the corkscrew. She opened the fridge, saw the plate of olives and cheese with a bowl of nuts in the centre and grabbed it along with some biscuits. When she saw Stephen sat at the dining room table with a pad of paper, pen and address book she nearly dropped the plate in shock. Alice sat down in her chair and took the glass of wine Stephen handed her.

Stephen looked at Alice intensely then half smiled, half grimaced, 'Hard work this and I haven't even put anything on paper yet. I was gonna use the computer but somehow it didn't seem right to type a letter like this.'

'You've got lovely handwriting anyway Stephen and I think a handwritten letter is somehow so much more personal.'

'But, where do I even start? It's been a lot of years.'

'How 'bout with Dear Mum and Dad?'

'Very funny. Anyway I told you I'm only writing to mum. Dad won't care for a letter from me, he couldn't get rid of me fast enough when I was seventeen.'

'But he didn't know what he was missing then, did he? You were a rowdy teenager and he wasn't a very patient father. That party you had where their house got trashed was, rightly or wrongly, enough to tip him over the edge. Maybe he has had long enough to realise his mistake? Just think how you would feel if you and Marcel had a big fight and he vanished on you?'

'Awful! But, my dad kicked me out, I didn't leave because I wanted to. The thing is Alice, my dad was always so needy of mum's attention. He was never able to give me unconditional love. All kids have parties that get out of

199

control, it's part of growing up and learning who you can trust. My dad spent my whole life making sure I learned that if anything went wrong, it was my fault. I can't imagine that's changed. But, just in case, I'll write the letter to them both. I think it would be safer to only put mum's name on the envelope though.' Stephen's voice took on a nervous edge though he left the rest of his fears unspoken and Alice wisely left the topic there.

'How about saying something like you know it has been a long time since you've spoken but you wanted to let them know what you've done in the time since you last saw them? Tell them about Marcel. You'll have no problem writing about Marcel.'

'Yes, that's true. Or about you, my other favourite topic.' Stephen smiled at her and reached out to smooth a finger over her wedding band then paused there for a moment with his hand over hers while he took a fortifying drink of wine. Eventually, after a few drafts, Stephen ended up with :

19 Bankshedge Close
Landsdown, Southampton
Hants, SO32 5TU

Dear Mum and Dad
I expect this letter will be somewhat of a surprise for you. I can only hope it is a pleasant one. I know we've not spoken for over 20 years and I think that it is time to try and put an end to our silence.

I have grown up now and I hope you have forgiven me for whatever things I did that you felt were awful enough to kick me out. All I can remember is a party I had that made dad go a bit nuts and kick me out but I am sure there must be more to the story. I am a father myself now and I couldn't imagine kicking my son, Marcel, out just for that but I also know that I would feel wretched if Marcel never spoke to me again.

Marcel is the main reason I am writing to you I suppose. Him and my wife Alice. Marcel has taught me a lot about the sometimes silent depth of parental love and of forgiveness. He'll be nine in January and has started to ask questions about you both now. Questions which made me realise I didn't have satisfactory answers. I would like Marcel to have a chance to know you both and Alice has encouraged me to sit down and take this first step with you both. I would like to hear from you. If you are interested too then you can write to me at the address on the top of the page.

Your son, Stephen

Stephen tucked in a family photo of the three of them and the cat and addressed the envelope to his childhood home hoping his parents still lived there.

'I'm cursing myself for my stubbornness now hon,' he said to Alice.

'What do you mean?'

'Now that I've written this letter I'm desperate for it to get to them and I have no idea if they still live in the same place. I wish I'd kept tabs on them, what if they've moved away?'

'Let's deal with that problem if we have to sweetie. We can look for them on the housing register online, put an advert in the paper, on the radio, there are lots of things we can try if we have to.'

'I'm going to walk to the post box now, we got any first class stamps?'

Alice took one from the booklet in her handbag and passed it to him, 'I'm proud of you darling. Really proud to be married to such a magnificent man.'

'You know I love you more than I can ever explain, don't you?' Stephen smiled at Alice and gave her a kiss. As he walked to the post box he knew that he was scared. He'd just taken a massive step into a reality which he'd visited before and not enjoyed on the whole. *What the hell am I doing?* he wondered. The letter felt hot enough to burn a hole right through his hand. He stopped and considered ripping it to shreds, pretending that he'd never written it but the late October cold got him moving again. Stephen posted the letter into the red pillar box and waited until he heard it land on top of the post already inside.

Three weeks passed. Three long weeks in which Stephen alternated between fretting because his parents hadn't responded, worrying that the letter hadn't got to them, and stomach sinking angst that perhaps the letter had been received but they had chosen not to respond. Alice worried that Stephen hadn't posted the letter at all for she couldn't entertain the concept of parents ignoring a letter like the one he had written. There was, of course, always the possibility that they had moved home and she suggested that Stephen give it another week before they put an ad in the Bournemouth news.

Three weeks and one day after Stephen posted the letter to his parents, Alice made a detour home after work on her way to collect Marcel from school, to see if Loopy wanted in. He was getting old and while her two were fine outside all day she did worry when Loopy refused to come in before she left for work. It could take an hour or more to collect Marcel on Mondays as that was the day they went to the library and Alice knew she'd keep worrying about poor old Loopy if she didn't let him in before the school run. Alice collected the post from the foyer floor and found an envelope addressed in an unfamiliar handwriting amongst it. She turned the lightweight envelope over in her hands looking for clues that this was from Stephen's parents. The return address matched his parents' one. Excited, hopeful and ever so slightly nervous for Stephen, Alice placed the envelope on top of the fridge for him to see when he got home from work that evening.

Stephen waited until Marcel was in bed and Alice was chin deep in the bath before opening the letter from his parents. He'd been glad of the excuse to wait because such a large part of him believed that what was inside the envelope had to be a rejection. *Why else would it have taken mum and dad three weeks to get back to me?* he wondered. Eventually, after turning the letter over and over, handling the envelope until it had become warm, soft and pliable, Stephen took a knife and slit the letter open along the top edge.

9 Edenbridge Crescent,
Locksway, Portsmouth,
Hants, PO4 8LK

Dear Stephen

Your dad and I were delighted to get your letter when we returned home from our holiday. We've been on a cruise to Alaska to celebrate your dad's retirement. Your letter must have arrived shortly after we left and I'm a bit worried we'll have lost this chance with you because it has taken us so long to answer your letter.

Your dad is a different person now. He was diagnosed with bipolar disorder several years ago and it took quite a long time to get his medication adjusted exactly right but it was worth the effort. I've got the man I married back now and I am grateful for it.

We've missed you a lot over the years Stephen but didn't think you would ever be able to forgive us for kicking you out. It was the wrong way to react to your behaviour and I have regretted allowing it to happen for many years. I tried to find you so many times over the years but you seemed to have vanished. I'd love to know what you got up to all these years, besides becoming a father and a husband which are wonderful accomplishments.

We've put the photo you sent up on our fridge. Marcel is such a handsome boy, we are proud grandparents already! We'd love to know more about him and your beautiful wife Alice. I do hope we can meet up soon, your dad and I are free all the time now our time is our won so we'll fit in around you. I'd best go now as your dad wants to say something to you.

Love, Mum xx

Son,

Your mum says I need to apologise to you and she is

203

right. I'm sorry for not being a better father to you, I tried but my bipolar got in the way. I know it's not an excuse but maybe you'll accept that is a reason for the way I treated you. I'm proud of the man you've become and I hope you'll feel able to say the same about me someday.

Dad

Stephen put the letter down and wept. Alice heard his sobs and with ice in her stomach she leapt from the bath pausing only to wrap a towel around her before rushing to Stephen.

'Sweetie! Oh Stephen.' She knelt down beside the couch and wrapped her arms round his chest. Alice could feel the weight of Stephen's head as he rested it on hers, fresh sobs wrenching their way out of him. Alice's eyes welled in sympathy. 'What did they say?' she asked when he'd finally stopped crying.

Stephen handed her the letter with a watery smile 'Read it,' he whispered and helped her up so she could settle herself on the couch before reading the letter.

Alice looked over at Stephen when she'd finished reading, 'Oh Stephen,' she said. 'So many answers on one sheet of paper. You ready to meet up with them now?'

'Yes if you'll come with me.'

'I'd love to.'

'But, not Marcel straight away.'

'That's fine Stephen, we'll go at your pace and introduce Marcel to them when you feel ready.'

Epilogue
20 years later

Marcel and Eddie Copeland are proud to announce the finalization of the adoption of their beloved daughter Jenniefer Alicia. The proud grandparents, Stephen and Alice Copeland and Frank and Joy Hutnick will be hosting a celebration evening of entertainment on the 8th March at St Ives community centre from 12-4pm.

Marcel looked down at the invite that was centred perfectly on the front cover of the memory album. He sunk into the chair gratefully, completely shattered from the long emotional day and flicked idly through the first several album pages. Each one had a sheet of paper proudly displaying a message from a friend or family member:

Condolences on the loss of your freedom! Kath and Tony P.S. Just joking, congratulations. Really! XXX

Welcome to the sleepless club, remind us to give you the number of all the kid's TV channels. Love Janet and Dave

Be careful, having children is addictive. You have been warned. Love Trish, Pat, Billy, Ivy, Charlie, Peter, and 'Baby in progress'.

Congratulations and remember that we'd be happy to babysit Jenniefer once in a while. Love you loads, Cam and Dom

Oh 'fer Chrissakes! I can't ever think of anything clever to write in these sorts of things. Congrats to all three of you. Chris

We're so happy that the most perfect couple we know just became the most perfect parents ever! Love Nanny and Pops Hutnick

Eddie had taken an overtired Jenniefer up to her room for the bath and bedtime ritual. Marcel had drawn the short straw, meaning he had to stay downstairs to keep the last of their lingering guests company instead of luxuriating in the milky scent of his sleeping daughter in the quiet of her room. Most of his and Eddie's friends had cleared off home from the community centre to put their own children to bed. Marcel's parents and one set of grandparents had followed them home and, as they were most of his family, Marcel didn't feel he could complain. Eddie's parents had left with Grammie Sabi and Grampie Art who'd offered them use of their spare room for the weekend. Grammie Fern and Grampie Gary, suffering from the combined effects of jet lag and daytime champagne indulgences, had made their way up to bed in the study which did occasional double duty as the spare room at 8pm.

'Oi, oi ref!' shouted Stephen at the TV. He was watching a late rugby game with Great Grandad Tim who always seemed to bring out the loutish side of Stephen's personality. Marcel's face softened as he watched his father for a long moment. His dad was the living embodiment of the term *contradiction*: gentle and loving towards his family though outwardly brash and outspoken at times. Never shy in coming forward with his opinion, his dad had plenty to say on how he felt Marcel should best conduct his life though this was always balanced by firm rebuttals from Alice and Sabi. *Perhaps all fathers do,* Marcel thought. He had often wondered, but never asked, if his father went over the top in his swaggering behaviour in order to try and disguise the softy inside. One thing Marcel had never doubted was that his father loved him wholeheartedly. His mind jumped to the moment today when his father had given him the book of memories that he'd secretly jotted down for Marcel throughout his childhood. The book was an absolute treasure and he knew he'd do the same for Jenniefer as she grew up. Eddie said he was very lucky to have such assuredness that he was loved. Marcel had never looked at it like that while growing up, since whether or not he was loved never came into question in his mind. Sure his dad had loads of opinions about how Marcel should conduct himself, what clubs he should join, why dancing was not a sport but rugby was and so on. But outwardly disapproving or not, his father had turned up to every dance recital that Marcel had ever performed in and Stephen had always been the first to lead the audience in a standing ovation when Marcel's performances were over. It was his dad who had driven him to and from London on a weekly basis while he attended the academy of arts to study dance at a professional level, his dad who worked extra shifts so that Marcel didn't have to work part time while focussing on honing his craft, and his dad who hugged him the tightest when he was offered his first job as a choreographer and dance instructor. Stephen always said that Marcel was a 'Mummy's boy', but both of them implicitly knew that Marcel really was a 'Daddy's boy'. *That's not to say that I don't adore mum*, Marcel corrected himself as he watched her glide into his line of vision to give his dad a peck on the top of his head.

'Gerroff woman!' Stephen always blamed Alice's kisses for balding his head, to which she'd swiftly counter with, 'Better to have your hair kissed away than lost through stress.' Marcel thought that pretty much described Alice perfectly, he'd never met anyone as full of love as Alice, and he treasured her. He knew that his dad and mum had had what they described as a 'rocky start' and that she wasn't his birth mother, but she was the only mother he could remember. His Grammie Sabi did her best to help him feel as if he knew his Jennie-mum and made occasional comments about how much Alice had changed his father for the better.

Once, when a teenaged Marcel had stayed with Grampie Art and Grammie Sabi when his parents were away for the weekend, she'd had a glass of wine too many. This loosened her tongue enough to start telling Marcel how much she'd hated his father while he was married to Jennie, because, although he'd been a good father, he'd never seemed to behave like a good husband. Grampie Art had interrupted her mid-flow to ask Marcel to get him another beer from the kitchen.

'What? Some wounds never heal no matter how long they've been scabbed over!' Sabi's voice was audible all the way into the corridor to Marcel's reluctant ears as he walked to the kitchen.

'There's some things that boy has no need to know,' Art answered in a tone of voice that made it clear he wouldn't argue any further.

If there was anything else said it was done with by the time Marcel had returned with Art's beer and a glass of cherryade for himself. Sabi and Art were cheerfully pouring over holiday catalogues, since they were planning a cruise for their next holiday. They ended the evening with a look through old photographs of Jennie, with Grammie Sabi telling the same stories she'd told many times before, and pointing out which Redwood family traits Marcel had inherited. Marcel was relieved that Grampie Art had successfully stopped Grammie Sabi as her words had made him squirm. He didn't like anyone criticising his dad, not even if he deserved it. Marcel was sure that his dad had learned how to be a good husband because he had never seen Alice anything but happy with his father. In fact, Alice liked to say that Stephen was a better man that he would ever admit, and that it was her job as his wife to one day convince him of that fact. *She's certainly made it her life's mission*, Marcel thought; that and being the best mum I could ever have wished for. His eyes unexpectedly welled with tears just as Stephen glanced back at him.

'I know son, I'm gutted they lost too but it's only a game, you shouldn't wear your heart on your sleeve like that.'

Marcel laughed, walked over and grabbed his dad in a mostly unreciprocated hug. His dad was still not entirely comfortable with adult male physical contact and probably never would be.

'I love you dad.' Stephen grunted and patted Marcel roughly on the back.

'Ah look at the pair of Nancy boys over there!' shouted Great Grandad Tim.

Stephen stepped away from Marcel and laughed. 'Careful dad or you'll be getting one and all!' Stephen mock-threatened before heading in the direction of the downstairs toilet, swatting Alice on the bottom as he tried to pass. She grabbed him by the jaw and kissed him before letting him carry on past her.

'It's high time we were heading home,' Alice said to the room at large when Stephen returned.

'Righty ho, if you insist,' said Stephen's dad. He took his coat from Marcel, and then on autopilot he went to hold it out so his wife could shrug it on. He looked a little lost as he always did when he remembered that she had died the year before last. The sight of his grandfather weeping at the funeral and muttering, 'It should have been me Babs, it should have been me,' was one that had disturbed Marcel's dreams for a long time after.

'Why don't you stay at ours tonight dad? Alice is making pancakes tomorrow and I could do with a hand sorting the shed after.' Stephen's soft expression was at odds with his jovial tone. Marcel knew it was because his Great Grandad Tim wouldn't stand for any of what he described 'mamby pamby sympathy'.

'I guess I'd better stay to make sure you don't change your mind about getting on with that. High time you made inroads into that mess,' Stephen's dad said, and managed a watery smile.

Eddie came running down the stairs in time to hug everyone goodbye, and after they promised to come round as soon as Jenniefer woke the next morning, they were finally able to close their door and allow the silence of their house to embrace them.

'A last glass of wine or bed?' Eddie asked after they had shared a luxurious moment of peace wrapped in each other's arms.

'Both.' Marcel put together a tray to take up to their room while Eddie tidied away the last signs of their memorable

209

day.

Lightning Source UK Ltd.
Milton Keynes UK
04 August 2010

157888UK00001B/4/P

Have you ever had a secret? One so important that it feels as if it will tear you in two? Stephen's got one. He's also got a great job, beautiful wife and an adorable son. Outwardly his life seems perfect but it means nothing without Alice. Read *Without Alice* and meet a man who you will love to hate until you learn to love him.

"I loved this book. DJ Kirkby is a gifted storyteller who draws you in with her silky narrative – then tightens her grip, forcing you to face uncomfortable truths"

Diane Hayman, Powder Room Graffiti

Cover image © Yuri Arcurs/Dreamstime.com

Published by Punked Books
www.authortrek.com/punked-books

Fiction UK £7.99 US $15.99

ISBN 978-095331726-4

90000

9 780953 317264